To Err is Azrin

Mission 4 of the
BLACK OCEAN
Series

J.S. Morin

To Err is Azrin
Mission 4 of: Black Ocean

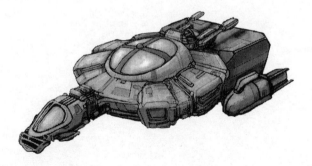

The crew of the *Mobius*:

Bradley Carlin "Carl" Ramsey (Human, Male, 32): Captain of the *Mobius*. Former starfighter pilot who left Earth Navy under questionable circumstances. Smuggler and petty con man with a love of ancient rock music.

Tania Louise "Tanny" Ramsey (Human, Female, 31): Pilot of the *Mobius*. Former marine drop-ship pilot and Carl's ex-wife. Daughter of a notorious crime lord who joined the marines to get away from her family.

Mordecai "Mort" The Brown (Human, Male, 52): Ship's wizard. On the run from the Convocation, he serves in place of the *Mobius'* shoddy star-drive. "The" is his legal middle name, a tradition in the Brown family.

Rodek of Kethlet "Roddy" (Laaku, Male, 45): Ship's mechanic. Laaku are a quadridexterous race with prehensile feet, evolved from a species similar to the chimpanzees of Earth. Never to be found without a beer in hand, he keeps the cobbled-together *Mobius* running.

Mriy Yrris (Azrin, Female, 16): Ship's security. The azrin are felid race who still hunt for their food. Despite her lethargy and slouching posture, she is a ferocious warrior.

Esper Theresa Richelieu (Human, Female, 24): Former initiate priestess of the One Church. She tried to do the right thing the wrong way, and it cost her a place in the hierarchy. Though she's signed on with the Mobius, she's still not sure what role fits her best.

Kubu (Species Unknown, Male, Age Unknown): A sentient dog-like creature, rescued from an illegal zoo.

The bounty hunter's ship swerved around a derelict hulk, dodging fire from the *Mobius*. The chase had started out entertaining when the *Remembrance*, thinking he was making his exchange, dropped out of astral. It wasn't ten seconds before he opened fire, ignoring hails as he fled into the Kapos IV scrap yard. But once a lucky shot had knocked out the bounty hunter's auto-cannon, it had devolved into fox-hunt.

As near as Carl Ramsey could figure, the captain of the *Remembrance* had few options. Curious whether his quarry had the same list in mind, he keyed the ship-to-ship comm. "Vessel *Remembrance*, this is Captain Michael Jagger of the independent ship Rolling Stone. It's time to consider handing over that cargo of yours while you've still got some leverage to negotiate. You won't shake us long enough to go astral. You won't get us to crash in the scrap-yard debris. It's time to hand him over before we accidentally blow out your life support or breach your hull."

"*Burn in hell, Jagger,*" came the curt response.

Carl clucked his tongue and shook his head. "Such disrespect for a noble musician." Of course, with the comm closed, the captain of the *Remembrance* didn't hear that.

"Probably too busy evading us to care," Tanny replied from the pilot's seat. It was her handiwork that kept the *Mobius* on the bounty hunter's tail.

"He's wasting his time," Carl muttered. With his arms crossed and feet up on the console, he knew he was far from the model of efficient time use, but his ship was winning. Winning bought a captain a bit of leeway.

Tanny twisted the *Mobius* on its axis and they swung around the hull of an Earth Navy light cruiser. There was a hole the

5

size of a small asteroid in the side—anti-matter torpedo, if Carl had to guess—and the *Remembrance* darted through it. The *Mobius* struggled to stay in the turn, but slipped through close behind. There was no sensation, no G-force tugging Carl from his seat—he wasn't even buckled in. Tanny flew with the safeties engaged. Between the thrust limiters and Mort's top-notch artificial gravity, her flying felt no different from sitting on a landing pad.

Carl yawned. If he were piloting, they'd not only have caught up with the bounty hunter's Osprey-class patrol ship, but they'd have had some excitement doing it. A staccato burst of plasma bolts shot across the forward window, narrowly missing the *Remembrance*. Mriy was picking at it with the guns, not wanting to destroy the ship outright. But it was damnably annoying to watch, knowing they were stuck giving chase until the azrin could land a lucky shot and take out the engines.

"Maybe we should give Esper a chance on the guns," Carl grumbled.

"Yeah," Tanny replied. "Same girl who won't fire a blaster and pulls her punches in Krav Maga sparring."

"I was joking," Carl replied deadpan. "Might not hurt letting Roddy have a crack at it though. He wouldn't—"

"Can you just shut up?" Tanny snapped. "This isn't as easy as it looks."

"Of course, you know," Carl said. "If you're having trouble, I can take over. You'd do a lot better than Mriy in the gunner's seat."

Tanny snorted. "We've got this won. We're just running him down now."

Carl cringed. It was the sort of thing that just wasn't said. Overconfidence bred carelessness. Thinking one step ahead could cause you to stumble over the one you were standing on. Plus, it was just plain old bad luck.

On the other side of the holey cruiser, the bounty hunter swung around. The cargo hold of the *Remembrance* opened, and something small and silvery tumbled out. Of course, at a quarter kilometer or so, "small" was a relative term. The fleeing ship changed course again, heading away from the vector of the cargo it had dumped.

"All yours," the captain of the *Remembrance* snarled over the comm. *"You can come after me or it, but it's headed for the munitions dump."*

Tanny checked the tactical sensors. "Shit! He's right. We can't—"

The *Remembrance* exploded with a plume of ignited oxygen as Mriy connected with a salvo of hits directly to the crew compartment. Tanny swung the *Mobius* around on an intercept course.

Carl leaned over and keyed the comm to the gunner's turret. "We were all set, Mriy. He dropped the pod and was making a run for it."

"I know," Mriy replied. *"That was personal."*

Mriy strode through the common room, not pausing as she glanced at Mort's holovid. He was watching a historical recreation from his home world. It was factual, if she was any judge of human narrators. The good ones rarely interrupted the action to have someone tell old stories.

Mort looked up as she passed. "We get him?"

"Not yet," she replied.

Down in the cargo hold, Roddy was waiting with Esper, both standing ready in their EV suits. Roddy gestured with his upper set of hands as she approached, but with the EV helmet on, Mriy heard nothing of what the simian mechanic said. He seemed to realize this and removed the helmet. "You gotta either suit up or get out of here. We're intercepting the pod and bringing it in through the cargo bay door, not the airlock."

"Why wouldn't we just—"

"Out!" Roddy shouted. "We're on the clock. Get pissy later." She envied the laaku his ease with the human language, but her ears flicked at his tone.

Esper, still wearing her EV helmet, shrugged an apology. It was just like her to avoid confrontation. She was like a bird, quick to chirp and quick to flight. Mriy showed a quick flash of fangs to the both of them and made a hasty retreat back to the common room.

The door between had a small window, enough for Mriy to watch Roddy and Esper. Red light strobed, and a klaxon blared; it was loud even muffled by the steel door, warning that the air was being pumped from the cargo bay. Mort's holovid grew in volume as the wizard sought to drown out the annoying noise. Against the assault on her senses, Mriy flattened her ears against her head.

"... the Roman senate was growing wary of Caesar's rising influence..." the narrator droned on.

The klaxon faded as the air left the cargo hold, but the human-deaf wizard left the holovid blaring. "Turn that down," Mriy ordered. She fought the urge to attach a bodily threat to her command. Commanding Mort in the first place was an error of riled temper. The wizard's own counter-threats ran far fouler than her own, and she had little doubt he could carry them out.

"Don't make me geld you, wizard." "I'd have your claws turned to butter before you cut through my jeans."

She shuddered at the memory of that particular threat. A declawed azrin was no longer fit to be a warrior. She might still fight with blades or guns, but her hand-to-hand fighting would make her a jesting target among her own kind.

Her own kind. Mriy returned her attention to the cargo bay, and looked out the open cargo bay as the *Mobius* matched speed with the cryostasis pod. The wreckage in the salvage yard was the only reference to show how fast they were traveling.

The pod was a silvery, flattened sausage. It tumbled through the darkness, shimmering with the light of Kapos, the sun of the system by the same name. The silver sausage grew larger as Tanny tapped the maneuvering thrusters, allowing the pod to catch up now that the *Mobius* was ahead of it. As it turned over, Mriy caught a flash off the glass window, covering a quarter of one side of the pod. The glare made it impossible for her to see in at a distance. Indicator displays glowed below the window, a good sign even if she couldn't make out what they said. At least the cryostasis pod had power.

Roddy and Esper prepared an inflatable mattress—one of the useless wonders of the ship's clutter—and lashed it to the cargo ramp. Roddy must have been coordinating over the comm with Tanny, because the *Mobius* sped up, slowing the pod's arrival and lining it up such that it would not enter the ship so high above the mattress.

The pod landed without a sound, but the mattress burst beneath its weight as Mort's gravity took hold of it. Esper hit the controls to close the cargo door, and Roddy began harnessing the pod to attach the tow cable. Moments later, the klaxon began to sound once more, growing in volume as air returned to the cargo bay. Mort increased the volume of the holovid, but this time Mriy didn't care. She tore open the door and rushed down to check on the cryostasis pod and its occupant.

The metal of the cryostasis pod was cold enough to burn, as Mriy discovered when she reached out to touch it. The glass had frosted over with the ship's humidity. A status display panel was visible and functioning, but she didn't know enough about the device's workings to tell anything useful from it.

"So are you ready to tell us who's in it?" Esper asked. She tucked her EV helmet under an arm as she sidled up to Mriy.

"I don't know," Mriy replied. It was an answer she had learned from Mort, who could put so narrow an edge on a question that it would cut. Uncertainty was merely a form of ignorance.

"Come on. You can't expect us to believe you gave up a share of our next job when you had no idea who we were rescuing." Esper leaned around to interpose her face between Mriy and the pod. "Who do you *think* is in there?"

Mriy flattened her ears back. This one spent too much time listening to Mort. Esper knew the trick in that reply. "I would rather not say until I am sure. I would look foolish."

"Yeah," Roddy interjected. "That'd be a first around here." He hopped onto the pod, walking across its surface as if it were level ground. With one gloved foot, he wiped away enough of the frost to see the face of the occupant. There could be no mistake.

Mriy sighed and let her shoulders slump. The frozen form was azrin, with fur coloration not so different from her own. He was young, not quite yet adult, but few non-azrin would have been able to tell. He was large for his age and quite muscular. "This is Hrykii Yrris."

"Wait... as in Mriy Yrris?" Roddy asked.

"My nephew," Mriy confirmed. "Son of my brother Soora."

Esper swallowed. "The one you—"

"Killed," Mriy said, nodding. Now that she knew it was Hrykii, there was no avoiding the topic. "Yes, the same brother. Hrykii is the eldest of his generation."

"How'd you hear about this whole..." Esper paused, waving a hand over the cryostasis pod. In her quest for perfect words, she often resorted to gestures, which ruined the intended effect. Human languages had so many words that they tripped over one another. "Business."

"A friend of Hrykii contacted me," Mriy replied.

"Thought you were on the Class-A shit list back home," Roddy observed with his usual tact.

"I doubt I was his first choice," Mriy replied. She pictured Roddy bleeding on the cargo bay floor, his entrails sagging from a gut wound. The daydream helped her anger with him pass quickly. "How is he?" she asked, turning to Esper.

The human woman had already removed her EV suit's gloves, and was fiddling with a datapad, connecting to the cryostasis pod's computer. The thought of being sealed inside such a device made Mriy's stomach sour—access to your med scans, able to gawk at you, control over your very life.

"Hold on," Esper replied. "I'm downloading azrin metabolic baselines. The pod didn't have them installed. I mean, for starters, he's alive. Broken arm in three places. Most of his ribs are cracked. System is flooded with adrenaline and a..." Esper cleared her throat. "A zoological sedative."

Mriy nodded along with the overview. "He fought. He was not caught unaware."

A few quiet minutes passed, broken only by Roddy clearing space in the cargo bay and Esper continuing to poke at her datapad. "Aha! Here we go," Esper said. "Running your nephew's bios against azrin norms."

Mriy peered through the glass. "He was so small last time I saw him…"

"OK. Taking into account his stasis—which rules out metabolic readings—his toxicity results are clean aside from the two I'd noticed on my own. No brain trauma. No nerve damage. Estimated height… wow, 1.9 meters. Mass: 86 kilos. That sound about right to you?"

"He takes after his father," Mriy remarked absently. Soora had been over two meters tall and 130 kilos. Hrykii had time to catch up.

"Huh?" Esper said. "It says his estimated age is seven."

"Barely, at that," Mriy replied.

"I would have guessed more like fifteen or sixteen, honestly," Esper replied.

Roddy chuckled. "You don't know azrins, huh? Miss Omni didn't look up everything, I guess."

"What's that supposed to mean?" Esper asked.

"*I'm* sixteen," Mriy replied. "We don't waste half our lives in childhood like humans and laaku. It's a primate trait."

Esper's face went long, her eyes wide. "I had assumed I was the youngest on the ship."

"No," Mriy replied. She laid a hand on the cyrostasis pod. It was still ice cold, but the air in the cargo bay had begun to warm it. "Right now, that honor is Hrykii's."

"How do we wake him up?" Roddy asked, trying to peer over the edge of Esper's datapad.

"We don't," Mriy replied. "He is badly injured."

"I can just—" Esper began.

"No," Mriy snapped. "No magic. He is safe in the pod."

"Fine," Roddy said. "What *are* we doing with him, then?"

Mriy hunched over and turned away. "I need to speak with Carl about that."

Carl's quarters smelled foul, a mixture of seeping human fluids and improperly disposed meals. Her own quarters had a Devesson filter, which kept the air cleaner than anywhere else on the ship. Carl's habitat was particularly deplorable. It was only due to her pressing need that she ventured inside at all.

"You know," Carl said as soon as she opened the door. "You didn't have to fire on that bounty hunter. He'd already cut his losses and turned tail." He was sitting on his bed, tuning Roddy's double-necked guitar.

She closed the door behind her. "I slipped," Mriy lied.

"Bullshit, and we both know it," Carl replied. He was such an unusual human. Few sentients would confront an azrin in an enclosed space. Those who did usually had some plan for defense. Tanny kept a blaster by her pillow. Mort was a wizard, and the less said about how he might defend himself the better. Roddy had made it clear she wasn't welcome in his quarters. Esper and Kubu were too naive to be properly afraid of her. But Carl... he just seemed to operate with a certainty that she wouldn't lose her temper and tear his throat out with her teeth.

Today, at least, he was right.

"I need a favor," Mriy said, allowing Carl's pronouncement to stand. They were better off with the bounty hunter dead, and Carl realized that. He just disliked reminders of how little he was really in charge aboard his own ship.

"You're down a favor already," Carl pointed out. He strummed a chord on the guitar, wrinkled up his face, and resumed his adjustment to the strings.

"I can give up another job's share," Mriy offered. "We need to deliver Hrykii."

"Who?"

"The one in the pod," Mriy replied. "My nephew. I... assumed Roddy had commed you as soon as I left the cargo bay."

"Nope," Carl replied.

"Well, that's who it is," Mriy said. "I need to—"

"The answer is 'no,'" Carl said. He played a sad little series of notes on the guitar. "We're not your personal shuttle service, and we don't get work often enough for me to let you go two paydays in hock to the rest of us. It's not like we can just take out a loan, or buy on credit except a few places I'd really rather not. We don't get *paying* jobs, I can't afford fuel, and we're stuck planetside. Nobody wants to see it come to that. I'm sorry, but I hope you can see that—"

"Fine. Three jobs with no cut," Mriy said.

"Deal," Carl replied, accompanied by a grating rendition of the opening song of the Buy-or-Sell Show. "Where we taking Ricky?"

"H-Ri-kee-ee," Mriy pronounced for him. "And we're taking him home. Rikk Pa, Meyang."

Carl nodded. He leaned over and keyed the comm for the cockpit. "Hey, Tanny. New course. We're heading to Meyang so Mriy can get herself killed."

Mriy gnashed her teeth at Carl's flippant summation of their mission. She glared into his smirking face as she retreated from his quarters. If only he had been wrong.

Meyang VII, most often referred to simply as Meyang, hung in orbit around a white sun that appeared yellow from the surface and was in turn orbited by a pale moon. A ball of blue and green, with wispy white clouds swirling in the atmosphere, it was as familiar as a child's first picture book. It looked just like Earth.

Esper shook her head as she watched the planetary approach through the common room's domed ceiling. "It's practically deserted. Like everyone on Earth took a holiday out of system, and just a few people stayed behind to water the plants." Orbital space around Earth swarmed with traffic. At any given time, a hundred thousand ships clogged the space lanes between the thermosphere and Luna's orbit. And then there were orbital habitats, diplomatic embassies not allowed planetside, military posts, shipyards, astral gates, and solar collectors. But not Meyang. It was hard to pick out the occasional craft against the backdrop of the planet, the one exception being the massive Earth Navy battle cruiser that was the planet's main garrison.

Mort looked on with her. "Pretty, isn't she? You can almost forget it's the twenty-sixth century for a while, looking at a pristine world like that."

"You ever been to an Earth-like before?" Esper asked.

Mort shrugged. "A few. This is the least modern I've seen though. If it's possible, Phabian is worse than Earth; laaku have no cultural regard for nostalgia. Keru though, they had a nice little wizards' retreat out in the Ural Mountains... well, what Earth calls the Ural Mountains. Spent a week there, once, getting the processed air out of my lungs."

"I've never been," Esper replied.

Mort patted her on the shoulder. "It's nothing to be ashamed of. You grew up in Sol. Not a lot of cause to go out looking for other Earths when you've got the original."

"No, I mean I've never even been to Earth," Esper said, shaking her head. "I don't even know where the Urals are. I mean, I can find New York and Tokyo and maybe London—I think—but it's not stuff I think about much."

"Never been to Earth?" Mort echoed. "Good Lord, girl. We're going to have to fix that one of these days. Cradle of humanity. It's a weeping shame never to have been, especially for a girl from Mars. What were your parents thinking, neglecting your cultural education like that?"

"They were thinking that Earth was a pretentious, snooty, over-regulated museum, not fit for regular folks," Esper replied. "What's Earth got that Mars hasn't?"

Mort snorted and rose from the couch. "What's Mars got..." he muttered. "I could write a book..." He sulked off toward his quarters. "... damned Martian bigots."

Esper thought that she was going to be watching the rest of the approach by herself. Meyang grew larger each minute. Such a grand sight seemed a shame to watch alone. Briefly, she considered seeing if Kubu wanted to come out and watch, but he was napping in Tanny's quarters.

"Here you go," Mort said as he opened the door from his quarters. In one hand he carried a cantaloupe-size ball that looked just like Earth. In fact, as Mort brought it closer, it might have looked *too* much like Earth. It wasn't plastic or fabric, but appeared to be actual rock and water, with a thin mist of clouds that spilled at the edges where Mort's hand held it.

When Mort pressed the orb into her hands, Esper found that it was no illusion. The surface was rough or wet in all the places it appeared it should be. The polar regions were even cool to the touch. "What is this?" she asked, hoping for an answer beyond the obvious.

"Best map I've ever owned," Mort replied. He leaned over the globe as Esper held it like a platter. "Ural Mountains."

The globe spun in Esper's hands, and a region that came to face Mort glowed softly.

"That's where they are?" Esper asked.

"Yup," Mort confirmed. "Go ahead and try it. You can't stump the thing."

Esper raised the globe to eye level. "New York Prime," she whispered to it. The magical map twisted around and a pinpoint of light brightened a coastal location.

"You don't have to add the 'Prime' on there," Mort said. "It knows you mean Earth. But watch... Phabian, Kethlet." The orb shuddered in Esper's hand, then twisted around and lit a small area on the far side from New York.

"What just happened?"

"I changed it to Roddy's world and his home district," Mort replied. "Roughly where Mumbai would be on Earth."

"Will it work here?" Esper asked. Mort's smile was all the encouragement she needed. "Meyang."

The globe vibrated, and this time she made sure to watch. The cloud cover reoriented instantly, and the colors changed, mostly to deeper greens. "Where's Mriy from?" she asked, not taking her eyes from the miniature planet in her hand.

"A place called Rikk Pa," Mort replied, enunciating with what sounded to Esper's ears like an attempt at an azrin accent. The globe spun around and lit a northerly area. "Looks like that would be somewhere in Norway, west of Oslo. Be cold as a polar bear's ass this time of year, too. They don't muck with the weather like Earth does."

Esper held the globe out to Mort, fearful of harming the priceless device if she kept it in her possession too long. "How's it work?"

"Damned if I know," Mort replied. "Probably some sort of magic."

The church held that the existence of Earth-likes was incontrovertible proof of God's hand at work. Every Earth-like's sun was a twin of Sol. Every moon identical to Luna. The extraneous orbital bodies in the system varied from one to the next, but every Earth-like spun in perfect synchronization. Mid November on Earth was still late autumn on Meyang's northern hemisphere, and it was indeed cold enough to warrant Mort's comparison to ursine posteriors. Getting used to different worlds was becoming a habit now, with how restless the *Mobius* was. Esper had no basis for comparing how close it felt to Earth, but it was a solid winter by Martian standards. Most spacers didn't risk damaging their EV suits by wearing them planetside, but she was glad of the warmth, despite the potential cost.

The ARGO-secure landing area was reserved for off-world vessels from ARGO member systems. With its Earth registry, the *Mobius* had no trouble passing the orbital security checkpoint or acquiring ground clearance for their choice of landing sites. After their adventures in the Freeride System and Hadrian IV, their easy entry to the system was something of a surprise. Meyang was an occupied world. Officially it was an ARGO protectorate, but that only meant that the Allied Races of the Galactic Ocean had claimed them before any of the galaxy's other powers could gain a foothold. The azrin had no status within ARGO in terms of citizenry or representation on the ARGO council. All around the landing area, there were reminders of that fact.

The landing zone was a roughly six-square-kilometer area, surrounded by a ten-meter wall and dotted with security towers. Patrol craft were in constant sight overhead, drifting around at low altitude; eyes looked down on all the naughty creatures below.

The crew piled into the hover-cruiser, an open-topped flatbed conveyance they had liberated from a previous job. Kubu was appointed Official Ship Guardian, which seemed appropriate, given that he was basically a sentient dog. There was a fine tradition back on Earth of using dogs to guard things, even if Kubu had the mental faculties of a preschooler. Convincing him to stay behind (and out of trouble) seemed the prudent course until they had a better idea of how he would be received on Meyang. The rest of them, along with the cryostasis pod, headed out to see Pikk Pa.

It was a short trip through the maze of parked starships and other small on-world transports. For that short while, there was the flickering possibility of an uneventful trip. But the security checkpoint at the exit stopped them.

"Sorry," an ARGO sergeant in articulated power armor informed them. He gestured to Mriy with a stun baton. "Cat's on the wrong side of the fence. This gate leads to the Humantown. No locals allowed." Esper could only imagine the security situation on a world like Meyang, where half the populace was deadly to even a seasoned soldier. Tanny's marine stories mentioned such armor for shock troops and front-line combat engagements.

"She's not technically a local," Carl replied from the front passenger's seat. He wore his battered leather jacket, but was otherwise girded against the cold in over-sized woolen mittens and a fur-lined hat with ear flaps. "She's part of the crew. And the popsicle isn't even conscious."

"I didn't notice your prisoner was azrin," the sergeant replied. "But in stasis, you can transport it. We're going to have to bring a shuttle for transporting your crewman. Can't have it in Humantown, whatever your relationship."

Mriy muttered something that Esper couldn't quite hear, but the guard obviously did. "Fine, you're a 'she.' Go ahead and fucking report me. I speak the local just fine, thanks."

"Sorry," Mriy muttered in English.

That drew a smile from the guard. "Well, at least you learned the language. Better than most of your friends around here. Fifty years... you'd think the schools would do a better job teaching it."

They waited fifteen minutes until a small official craft arrived, and Mriy transferred aboard. She went without complaint, climbing into the back of a craft with separate cockpit and passenger compartments. Even an angry azrin would have had difficulty disrupting the flight. The ARGO shuttle lifted off, and Esper watched to see whether Mriy might wave, or at least look down at them from the window. She didn't.

"Think she'll be all right?" Esper asked to no one in particular as the hover-cruiser zipped through the security checkpoint. They were cleared as soon as they were rid of the unauthorized azrin.

"Nothing to worry about," Roddy replied. "Just life on an occupied world."

Esper found it odd that no one gave a second look to the laaku as they headed for Humantown. Laaku were nearly human, and azrin were not.

Mriy sulked in the back of the shuttle. Her fur bristled in embarrassment, and she was glad that her crewmates were largely oblivious to those sorts of azrin subtleties. This was her world, not theirs. Yet because their ancestors had develops starships and plasma rifles and energy shields before her own, she was the one barred from certain areas of her home world.

The temptation to look down at Rikk Pa from the air nagged at her. The view from the *Mobius* on approach had been all too brief, and she didn't have a good vantage from her quarters. But the shuttle had a camera in the passenger compartment, watching her. She didn't want to look like a homesick reverse tourist, drooling at the evergreens and smoke-puffing chimneys through dingy transparent titanium. It was a matter of personal dignity, something that was all too hard to come by in the custody of the occupation force.

Had she been gone so long? Three years was a solid bite of her adult life, and she had grown used to human company. She understood their main language. How had she forgotten the feeling of being on the wrong side of the wall? How could a weakling race cordon off a tiny portion of Meyang, and yet make it feel like the azrin were the ones trapped? Smug tourists on her world, venturing into the azrin cities and building shops, hospitals, factories—as if they were some great force of civilization. Carl wasn't so bad. Tanny was nearly azrin, in some ways. Even Esper was more like a kitten than the invaders she had grown up around.

The pilot of the shuttle could mate with cows for all she cared. Mriy looked. Spread out below were water and mountains, with snow-dusted valleys in between. It should have come as no surprise, but she smiled at the realization that she knew the names of these places. Kinna Peak, gray and imposing. The Godswash, flat as a mirror, reflecting the clouds above. Here and there, little clusters of homes and businesses—a dozen here, a hundred there—with forest and roads stitching them together to form Rikk Pa.

"Down in two," the pilot's voice buzzed over the comm. He was just three meters away, but on the other side of a safety-grade wall of composite steel and transparent titanium. She'd be rid of him in two minutes, plus however long the departure sequence took.

Public terminals were a good deal shabbier than the landing site for ARGO-registered transports. Asphalt tarmac instead of evercrete. No security fence. Just a lone navigation control tower and ground tram service up and down the rows of mismatched ships. In fairness, the *Mobius* would have fit better here than among the up-to-spec vessels in the high-security zone, but registry was everything. As for Mriy herself, she was of Meyang origin; her registry said this was where she belonged, locked out of the safe zone for humans.

As she hopped down to ground level, Mriy wished she had taken some personal effects. This had only been intended as a drop-off followed by a quick return, but Rikk Pa tugged at her. She might not be welcome, but she was in no hurry to leave, either. Returning to the *Mobius* no longer promised to be such a quick trip. Carl was likely going to have to come back and pick her up outside the security zone when it was time to leave.

If she was going to leave.

It wasn't a foregone conclusion that she was going to survive her homecoming. Bad blood among humans might run cold under the watchful stare of the law. But here she was under no such protection. There were several azrin who were well within their legal rights to kill her, including Hrykii, once he was thawed.

But none of that was worth dwelling on. It would happen, or it would not. She couldn't very well show up to the family compound without her nephew, which meant meeting up with the rest of the crew. Tanny's tactical brief before they arrived had included Mriy selecting a rally point in case they became separated. This wasn't the circumstance Mriy had envisioned when planning things out, but then again, that's what Tanny's contingencies were for—dealing with the unforeseen.

Following signs written both in Jiara and English, Mriy made her way to the ground transport station. A brown-furred attendant greeted her.

"Where will you be when you arrive?" he asked. He had an odd accent and manner of speech. He was Ruuthian, a long way from his home on the far side of Meyang.

"Nowhere far," she replied. "There's a cluster of off-worlder restaurants by Humantown. How much?"

"Eight dreka," the attendant said.

Mriy dug in her pockets for local currency. It had been a long time since she'd bothered carrying drekas. Filtering through a pile of cubic metal blocks, she found a two-by-two-by-two and passed it across the counter. The attendant picked up the coin, looked it over, and tossed it into a jar with a clink. A digital display read 008 momentarily, before going blank.

"Bay Three," the attendant told her.

The vehicle that awaited her was an old model Capchak dirt-roller. Its metal tracks were rusted and pitted, but otherwise looking sound. It didn't matter much how badly it ran. If a dirt-roller broke down, the riders could just walk away. It wasn't like a starship, or even a hover-cruiser in that regard. The engine growled like a warrior's challenge, and the driver popped out of the forward hatch to wave. "Climb on. Ziyek called ahead. Ready to roll when you're up."

The driver was all black, with three links of chain dangling from one ear. His fur bushed out at the neck, making him look stronger than he probably was. But right now, Mriy found her chest heaving. It had been a long time with no male companionship—non-azrin hardly counted. The driver obviously had no idea who she was; he was probably barely grown when she'd left. If they had known one another before, both had changed in the intervening years. It was possible... no, as soon as he discovered who she was, it would end badly.

Slowing her breathing with a human concentration technique, Mriy hauled herself over the side railing of the dirt-roller. "Roll when you wish," she shouted. The wind of speed and weather combined to cut through her vest and fur, straight to the bones. The dirt-rolled gouged its way across Rikk Pa's landscape, and Mriy's body let loose the heat of anxiety, anger, and starship environmental furnaces into the Meyang atmosphere. Throwing back her head, she let out a roar. Whatever lay ahead for her, at that moment, she felt more alive than she had in years.

❀ ❀ ❀

"You've got to be kidding me," Esper said as they reached the rendezvous point.

Carl chuckled. "You've got to get planetside more often."

The location Mriy had chosen was just outside Humantown, in an area where human-curious azrin congregated. The restaurant where they would wait for her was called Human Joe's Cow Ranch. It featured an actual ranch out back, with doomed bovines milling around and a gaudy holovid of an azrin in a cowboy outfit playing on loop over the roof.

Esper ended up at the front of the group and pushed her way through the saloon doors. "I'm just going to take a wild swing and say that azrin's name isn't really Joe," she said, raising her voice over the piped-in frontier music. The inside of the eatery was just as overblown and tacky. Giant cow and bull heads adorned the wall, mounted like hunting prizes in old-Earth fashion. The tables and booths surrounded a dirt-floor arena, where a robotic bull stood idle. "What's going on down there?"

"Looks like we're about to find out," Tanny said. There was a queue of azrin at the entrance to the arena, and the attendant opened the gate to allow a lone azrin through.

"Can I seat you, partners?" a white-furred azrin asked. His accent was a distinct attempt at an old-Earthish dialect consistent with the décor. With his cowboy hat, holstered six-shooters, and spurred boots, he didn't look much like a restaurant host. The stack of menus he carried said otherwise.

"We're meeting someone," Carl replied. Having spent time around Mriy, Esper picked up on the subtle shift in the host's ears, signaling annoyance. The polite smile never left his face though—probably part of his training for dealing with human customers.

"Got a bar?" Roddy asked.

Whether it was an intentional effort on Roddy's part to appease the host, or—more likely—simply a desire for a beer or five, the host perked up. "Of course, sir. Follow me."

The bar was packed, and despite a preponderance of azrin customers elsewhere in the restaurant, most of the barflies were human. Drinking for the sake of it was a cultural export that just hadn't caught on, at least on Meyang. Roddy pushed his way close enough to get the barkeep's attention and bought a round for the crew.

Down in the arena, a tan-furred azrin was stripping off his vest and approaching the robotic bull. A loudspeaker blared overhead. "Next contestant, Uajiss Finnu." It was hard to get a sense of scale with nothing near the lone azrin besides the bull. The would-be bullfighter was heavyset, with a swaggering walk that suggested confidence. He raised his arms and spread his fingers with claws extended—not that those thirty-millimeter blades would help against his robotic opponent.

A horn sounded and the bull charged. Esper had never seen a live bull up close, but this false one acted enough like a living creature that she was willing to give it the benefit of the doubt as a plausible reproduction. It shook its shoulders and thrashed its head as it bore down on its azrin challenger. The bullfighter sank into a ready crouch, an easy posture for the feline legs of an azrin. With whisker-thin timing, the challenger dodged aside as the bull careened past, angling stainless steel horns to gore.

Esper gasped along with a good portion of the human crowd. The azrin spectators hissed or looked on in silence. "What would happen if he didn't get out of the way?"

Tanny shrugged. "They got medics around here somewhere."

The bull pulled up and twisted around, aiming itself once more in the azrin's direction. With less room to build a head of steam, the robot came in slower, though exhibiting no less ferocity. This time when the azrin dodged aside, he grabbed one of the horns and held on. The bull flung its head back and forth, seemingly unsure whether to shake loose its opponent or try to impale him on the held horn. Despite the erratic movements, the bullfighter managed to catch hold of the other horn as well, holding the bull as if it were a bicycle or an anti-grav sled.

"Boo," Roddy muttered, slipping onto a seat at the bar while one of the patrons was distracted. "This guy's a pro. I was hoping we'd see some idiot get himself skewered."

Down in the arena, the robot and azrin wrestled for leverage. The bull pushed; the azrin put his feet back to maintain balance as he skidded along the dirt. The bull tossed his head; the bullfighter stretched long arms and legs to keep both his footing and his grip. The crowd cheered—a mix of human hoots and azrin yowls. Uajiss Finnu was putting on a show. Through remarkable programming, the robotic bull appeared to grow frustrated. It snapped its head from side to side, unable to shake its prey-turned-tormentor. On one pass, the bullfighter shifted his weight, overbalancing the robotic beast to one side. Hanging from the horns, he swung under the bull, kicking out one of the robot's legs with both of his and toppling the machine to the dirt.

The crowd's cheering reached a crescendo. Esper let out a sigh. "At least he didn't get hurt."

"Cut his arm," Tanny replied. The azrin stood atop the now inert beast. There was no thrashing, now that the program had run its course. Against the tan fur, there was a matted smear of red on one upraised arm. "Doubt he cares though."

Esper gave Tanny a narrow-eyed glare. "You're not thinking of—"

"*Hell* no," Tanny replied. "I don't think I've got the mass for it. And I certainly don't have anything to prove to *this* lot."

"I saw a sign at the entrance," Esper said. "There's prize money. Works out to about 7800 in terras."

Carl's eyes widened. "You know, Mort..."

"The answer is 'no,'" Mort replied before Carl could even get the question out. "I could reduce that bull to a flopping sack of loose parts, but I don't think anyone would believe I hadn't cheated. For Chrissakes, just look at me. Now look at the fella with his furry arms up in the air. Which of us looks like a likely candidate to flip robo-cattle on their asses?"

"Bet we'd get good odds," Carl replied.

"And get ourselves arrested. It's not even subtle," Esper said. She lowered her voice and tried to spice it with an angry edge. "And I'd thank you to keep those larcenous thoughts bottled up when we're out in public."

"Where's Mriy anyway?" Carl wondered aloud. "Shouldn't be taking her this long to cut across town. Where the hell'd those patrol twits ditch her? Off-world?"

Carl's answer came in the quieting of the crowd. There were places where the buzz of voices ebbs and flows to the point where an occasional quiet moment might have gone unnoticed. Human Joe's wasn't one of those. Curious eyes turned toward the entrance, where a lone azrin entered. White furred except for a few spots of orange, she stood tall and towered over most of the azrin around her. Esper hadn't realized that Mriy was so large a specimen among her own kind.

Mriy scanned the crowd until her eyes fell on the *Mobius* crew, then she headed their way. The crowd parted for her as whispers spread around the eatery. One brown-furred azrin stepped into her path, but a twitch of Mriy's lip to show fangs was enough to move him out of her way. Esper could only surmise the azrin's gender, of course. Accustomed to primate anatomy, she was largely ignorant of the clues to tell azrin sexes apart.

"Quite an entrance," Carl remarked as Mriy joined the group.

Mriy kept her voice low. "I hadn't expected to be recognized so quickly or easily. Can we get out of here?"

"Looks like you can clear us a path," Carl said. "Lead on."

Esper fell into step near the rear of an impromptu parade to the exit. Only Roddy came after her, carrying one of Human Joe's mugs as long as he could to drain its contents. It seemed as if the restaurant had paused while Mriy was inside. Whether it started up once more upon their departure, Esper could only speculate.

No one questioned Mriy when she took the controls of the hover-cruiser. This was her world, after all.

Dusk had settled over Rikk Pa by the time they arrived at the Yrris Clanhold. Mriy had hardly said a word on the trip, answering brief queries about the landscape and their destination with even briefer replies. Human Joe's had put her on edge. A whole restaurant full of people all knew she was back. Whether a few keen observers had spread word like an avalanche or every person on Meyang recognized her on sight, the effect was the same. Word would reach her family before Mriy did.

From the outside, the clanhold appeared unchanged since her youth. Evergreens along the winding road hid the compound from view until they were almost upon it. A dozen squat, conical buildings poked through the snow that coated the mountain lowlands, chimneys belching woodsmoke into the evening sky. It had been springtime when she'd last seen it; the herd grass was green and soft on bare feet. It should have changed more since then. There should have been a new house built, or one of the old ones burnt down. Even a few darkened buildings with no fires burning would have shown that the Yrris Clan had fallen on hard times without her.

"Looks cozy," Carl said, his words coming out accompanied by puffs of fog. He huddled in his jacket with his arms hugged close. "We gonna just look at it all night?"

Mriy bit back a snarl. It was no good arguing with Carl when he was wrong, let alone when he was in the right. She hit the accelerator and started the hover-cruiser toward the hearth hub, center-most building in the clanhold. The cheerful, inviting, mocking, spiteful lights from the windows grew closer.

Floodlights snapped on, blindingly bright, forcing Mriy to slow the hover-cruiser. Engine hums came from left and right, approaching and surrounding them. Snow-rollers revved their engines as they encircled the *Mobius* crew and Mriy was forced to either stop or risk hitting someone. She might have been able to put enough air under the craft to jump it over the snow-rollers, but that was a trick better suited to Carl's skill set, not her own.

"Heard you were back, Mriy," a voice shouted over the growls of combustion engines. "You're going to regret it."

"I came to bring back Hrykii," Mriy replied in the direction of the speaker. "You defend the clan now, Yariy?"

"Of course it fell to me," Yariy replied. "Who else? Soora? You?"

"Graida," Mriy answered.

"Dead."

"Seris?"

"Offworld, earning for the clan," Yariy said. "You said you had Hrykii. All I see are humans with you."

Mriy elbowed Roddy to keep him quiet. The last thing they needed was his surly tongue. She pointed to the back of the hover-cruiser. "In the tube. We rescued him from a bounty hunter. He is too badly injured for us to wake from stasis with no doctor. We brought him straight here."

A single snow-roller revved its engine, and Yariy pulled alongside the hover-cruiser. Standing on her vehicle's seat, she looked at their cargo and ran a hand along the smooth surface. "Get him inside. We'll see about you when we get the tale from him."

"But I thought—" Mriy said.

"You thought wrong," Yariy replied. "Seerii speaks here. I serve. You have no standing. We'll find you if Hrykii thinks you've earned a voice."

Mriy fumed in the night air. She would not have been surprised if the snow melted under her glare. Yariy had been a child when she left, and now gave orders like a guardian. For once the *Mobius* crew kept a respectful silence. She had dragged them into this, but they had no stake in Yrris clan matters. Two younger cousins hefted Hrykii's stasis pod between them and loaded it onto a snow-roller driven by someone Mriy had never met. The latter might have mated into the clan recently, or may have been a hired claw for all she knew.

The snow-rollers grumbled and kicked up white, powdery wakes as they sped off into the security of the clanhold. When they were out of sight, the floodlights went dark and the mystery of night set in.

"So, we done here?" Carl asked, shivering.

"For tonight," Mriy answered. "I can't easily go back to the ship, but the rest of you can. I'm going to stay in Rikk Pa."

"For how long?" Esper asked.

"If Hrykii vouches for my actions, perhaps forever."

As Earth-like worlds went, Meyang was sparsely populated. Carl might have gone so far as to call it deserted. While humans had bred Earth to the brink of ruin before spilling out into the stars, the azrin people had kept their numbers down to levels of pre-industrial Earth. There was unspoiled land between cities, and even a fair amount within them. Rikk Pa was more of a patchwork collection of villages, shopping centers, and civic hubs than any city Carl had seen. As Tanny parked the hover-cruiser, he and the crew prepared to do a little local exploration.

"Remember, keep your comms handy at all times," Tanny said, part of her standard security briefing for planetside romps. The reputation of the locals aside, Meyang ought to have been as safe as anyplace they'd been in a long time. As a protectorate, the planet warranted direct protection of the ARGO fleet. And since the azrin central government wasn't too keen on the idea, there were ground forces aplenty on the surface.

"Not it," Roddy called.

"Not it," Carl quickly echoed.

"Looks like it's your turn," Tanny said to Esper.

"Me? My turn for what?" Esper asked.

Mort chuckled. "You ever seen me carry a comm?"

"I'm babysitting?"

"Egads, girl, I could be your—well, I was about to say grandfather, but that might be stretching it a bit. Let's just say that I could be your father, and I don't need babysitting. Think of it as being a caddy for me, carrying a comm around in case Mother Hen needs to check under her britches to see if we're all still breathing and unmolested by the local constabulary."

"Fine," Carl said, interceding between the two. "I'll tag along for a while. Not like I've got money to blow on anything fun."

In daylight hours, Rikk Pa was brisk, not so bitterly cold as the night before had been. So while Roddy slunk away to find a bar with wide hours and Tanny flitted off on errands she wouldn't share, Carl fell into step behind Mort and Esper, taking his amusement in watching the two of them together.

"If this is the azrin section, why do all the signs have English, too?" Esper asked as they passed the civic tram depot.

"ARGO rules with an iron clipboard," Mort replied. "Rules with rules, so to speak. I doubt one in five can read them, but they put the signs up with both languages all the same. Next generation it might be one in four, then one in three. Sooner or later, grandparents will be teaching their children azrin so that they remember the old ways, and not the other way around."

"Worked for Roddy, I suppose," Esper said.

"Not hardly," Carl piped up. "Laaku are nearly all bilingual. They didn't give up their native languages; they just all decided to learn ours so we'd leave them alone about it. I think Roddy's got to know at least three or four."

"Six," Mort said. "English, plus three from his own world, a smattering of setrine, and he's picked up the major azrin dialect from Mriy. Ask any laaku and they'll tell you the same: they're smarter than us."

"Wow," Esper whispered. "I had no idea."

"Well, correct him on his grammar sometime," Mort said with a sneer. "Rotten monkey speaks better English than the lot of you when it suits him. He doesn't like people thinking he's stuffy, but you can egg him on until he proves it."

"Forget that crap," Carl interrupted. "Where we going?"

Esper looked back at him with a frown. Carl returned a sanguine grin. "I looked at the local map this morning, and there's a cathedral nearby that—"

"Oh, come on," Carl griped.

"That belongs to the One Church," Esper continued. "It's Saturday, so there won't be Mass. I'm just going to confession."

"Well, since you've been traveling with us for what, four months or something?" Carl asked. "You'll be in there a while."

"Very funny," Esper replied. "I'd say you need it worse than I do, but you don't care, and they wouldn't listen to you anyway. You have to actually be penitent to confess. You'd just be bragging."

Carl shrugged. She was right of course. "How about you, Mort? Anything you want to get off your chest?"

"If I'm of a mind to discuss my immortal soul, I'll address the man in charge directly," Mort replied with a huff.

The Cathedral of Saint Hubertus stood out amid the largely azrin architecture. Near as Carl could figure, everything around Rikk Pa was built to deal with heavy snowfall—steep roofs, elevated main floors, and underground passages to nearby buildings. The Cathedral of Saint Hubertus was Old Earth Gothic, complete with flying buttresses and gargoyles perched around the roof. If Mriy was any indication of her peers, that last detail was bound to go over well with the locals.

"Will you two wait for me?" Esper asked before heading inside.

Carl looked to Mort with a shrug, and the wizard shrugged right back. "Sure," Carl replied. "Make us wait long enough for my feet to start hurting though, and you're finding your own ride back to the ship."

They waited until the oak doors closed behind Esper. "So, what do you want to do while she's in there?"

34

Mort cleared his throat. "I think I'm going to see if they've got a washroom in there."

Carl watched Mort with a suspicious eye, wondering what he might be up to.

Esper stepped from an alien world into an embassy of peace and infinite love. It was unfair to say that if you had been to a single One Church cathedral you had been to them all, but there was a certain consistency to them. Same stained-glass iconography, even if the images varied. Same pews, with velvet upholstered kneelers. Same hymnals and Bibles. Same confessionals.

Esper's boots echoed on the polished floor, the marvelous acoustics carrying the sound throughout the nave. She gawked and meandered, letting a smile slip across her face as the warmth of home seeped into her. This was the real reason humans built cathedrals. They were old, solid, dependable. One cathedral was as close to the Lord as any other. He was always present, cathedral or no, but this was the reminder that He was omnipresent. You couldn't forget or dismiss His presence from within these sanctified walls. After months adrift and conflicted, Esper Theresa Richelieu felt her feet beneath her.

She was far from alone. There were worshipers scattered among the pews—mainly human, but a surprising number of azrin mixed with them. There was a confessional with the door slightly ajar, and she headed straight for it. The inside was darker than she was accustomed to, but that quaint musty smell of old wood in tight spaces brought a twitch of a smile.

A moment later, a priest sat down on the other side of the screen. "How long has it been since your last confession?" he asked.

Esper knelt and made the sign of the cross. "Bless me Father, for I have sinned. My last confession was six months ago."

"I hope you may find an easing of so long a burden," the priest replied.

Esper began with the gravest sin she had committed. "Father, though it was not my intent, I have killed a man." That was where it began. From there, the dam burst. Everything she had done since joining the *Mobius* and even the short while before poured out of her: her use of magic, her crimes against secular law, and her brushes with temptation of the flesh. The priest made scant comment throughout, allowing her to continue until she had to pause for breath.

"Of all these sins, which do you most fear?" the priest asked.

"Fear?" Esper echoed, not quite understanding this unexpected line of questioning.

"Did you find killing gave you pleasure? Did it sit easily on your conscience?"

"Of course not, Father!"

"Did you regret not acting when offered the pleasure of the flesh? Do you fear that you will succumb the next time, or the time after that?"

Esper paused. "Maybe a little. I try though, and so far trying has been enough. I pray for that strength."

"Did you enjoy the feel of handling God's power?"

"I... I've used it twice to save lives and once to take one," Esper replied. "I felt guilt each time, but maybe not as much when I helped people. I may have also overlooked this one, but I've also taken to using the hunger side effect of the healing spell to burn off chocolates so I can eat more of them. That one I always feel guilty about too—more for the magic, a little less for overindulging in chocolates."

"I will tell you something that may set your mind at ease," the priest said. "The powers you possess are a gift from God. The misuse of them is certainly a sin, but there can never be a more proper application of them than the saving of a life. But since you have also killed by negligence, I will enjoin you to study. If you would continue to serve your fellow man in the manner of Christ, you must separate the beneficial from the malignant. It is a burden you carry and a responsibility. Find a way to control and harness the goodness that resides within you, and be not ashamed of doing the Lord's work."

"That's my penance?" Esper asked.

There was a soft noise from the other side of the screen, too polite to be either a snort or a laugh, but suggestive of both. "I never said that. This goes beyond, and it will carry with you far longer. You must either give up the use of this power entirely, which would be a pity, or learn to use it with the certainty that it will do the good that you wish."

After that, the priest gave a long overview of the prayers she would need to recite, starting right then. He left her to her Hail Marys and her rosaries with an admonition to consider her choices when it came to giving up magic.

Mort strolled out of the cathedral with a grin that threatened to split his face in two. Carl checked the chrono built into his comm. "You get lost looking for that washroom, or did you get a little sidetracked along the way?"

As he walked by on his way to a wooden park bench, Mort snickered.

"You did it, didn't you?" Carl asked.

Mort shrugged. "I'm going to hell anyway."

"Come home."

That was all the note said. Mriy had waited all morning in her rented room at the Taste of Sol boarding house. It wasn't until she checked an old comm ID that she hadn't used in years that she finally discovered it. It was unsigned, and from a comm ID she didn't recognize—she wasn't the only one who had moved on in the years she'd been gone.

She considered calling Carl and letting him know where she was going, but decided against it. This was her business, not his. Besides, Carl wouldn't be pleased that she had a recording of their encounter with the *Remembrance*. But as Mriy clutched the data crystal, she knew it had been a wise precaution. Without her recording of the sensor feed from the chase and stasis pod recovery, it would have been her word alone as to what happened; Hrykii had been in stasis through the whole ordeal.

Without access to the crew's hover-cruiser, she booked a quick intra-city livery service to pick her up and take her home. It was human owned, but azrin operated. QuickRide hadn't been operating in Rikk Pa when she'd last been there, and it felt odd being chauffeured by a handsome young azrin in a human-styled suit, complete with sleeves.

There were no floodlights when she arrived at the Yrris Clanhold, no swarm of snow-rollers. Her boots crunched the snow as she waded to the main building's front door. How long had she lived there? How long had she lived away? Weighing her childhood against her professional travels and her exile, she had spent more of her life there than anywhere else. But those early memories were hazy. There was no warmth waiting for her, despite the chimney smoke that foretold a hearth fire.

She pounded her fist four times on the door. Four was the Yrris number, telling the door guard she was family. But Yariy was the one to open it, and Mriy wasn't sure Yariy considered her to be family at all. "You came after all," Yariy said, stepping aside to allow Mriy in.

"The message went to an old ID," Mriy replied. As she stepped past, she made sure not to slouch low enough to let Yariy seem even close to her own height. Though her cousin had a reputation in her own right, it was no time to let Yariy think she could be bullied.

"You left a lot of old things behind," Yariy replied. "Seerii didn't wait for you. She's out hunting for lunch."

"I haven't eaten," Mriy replied, dangling the implied offer to join the hunt. It was encouraging to hear that her mother was still fit to kill her own food.

"Maybe you should have thought of that before you came," Yariy replied, slamming the door. "We're not here to feed you. The hunting grounds are for the family."

"But I thought—"

"You thought wrong," Yariy snapped, taking a step to close the gap between them. It was a bold move, considering their difference in size. Mriy had come unarmed as a sign of good faith, and Yariy had two knifes at her belt. Mriy still liked her odds. Her cousin was shouting to tempt an avalanche. "Whatever Seerii decides, she hasn't told me anything about treating you like family."

Mriy took a step of her own. She loomed over her cousin and had the satisfaction of watching Yariy's ears flatten back. It was an easy thing to talk like the clan guardian when no one threatened to convert those words into actions. "A life for a life. Mother can't deny that. She might not forget, but she will forgive. And when she does, I'll be in my rights to challenge for your job as guardian. Think on that." She gave Yariy a shove and knocked her cousin back a step.

Yariy was a finesse fighter and a good one. She'd obviously improved in the years Mriy had been gone, or she wouldn't have risen to guardian. But that didn't mean she was a threat to Mriy. Yariy wouldn't have taken the guardian's job from Soora. Mriy had been nearly as strong as Soora, but too quick for her brother. She suspected she was just as nimble as Yariy and could throw her around like prey.

Yariy glared at Mriy, but took another step back. "What's wrong with you? You think you can barge in here, talking with a human accent, and buy forgiveness? You'd destroy the clan. No one would stay if you became guardian."

Mriy had never considered that she'd picked up an English accent.

"By rights, the job is mine," Mriy replied. She'd defeated Soora, and the unfortunate confrontation at the conclusion had earned her exile. But in that brief interim, she had owned the position. "If you don't win it from me, it's a hollow title."

Yariy flashed her teeth. "We'll see about that." She whirled and stalked out of the room. Over her shoulder, she called back, "Yesterday's kill is in the cold room. Stay out of the hunting grounds."

❁ ❁ ❁

It was another hour before the hunting party returned. Mriy had pillaged a lunch of venison after trying without success to discern by claw marks who had killed it. She used to know the habits and hand spans of every hunter in the Yrris Clanhold. Soora's handiwork was plain by the massive deep cuts in the prey's flesh, claws spread wider than any other Yrris. Her father had a penchant for snapping necks without leaving a scratch. Some younger cousin likely killed deer that provided her meal.

There were a lot of young cousins in the party that arrived back at the clanhold. Seerii led them. It gladdened Mriy to see Hrykii was well enough to have gone along. But aside from Meriik and Seninshee, the rest were strangers to her, grown children she no longer recognized. They walked past, ignoring her; four of them lugged a brown bear in a litter, already skinned. The four carried the animal into the butchery for preparation, without so much as a sidelong glance in Mriy's direction. It was Seerii who finally broke the shunning.

"You came back," her mother said. "I thought perhaps you would not."

Mriy stood and hung her head. Contrition was her best ally, now. "I belong here. This is home."

Seerii hissed softly. "Home is family, not a place. Soora understood, but never you. Settle down. Take a mate. Raise your children. Then you'll understand, too."

Mriy felt her hackles rise. "I'm too old to find a mate." It was a hard thing to admit with so many strange faces watching. She had wasted her best years away from Meyang, first fighting for money, then in exile. A family of her own was always a plan for later, until later became too late.

Seerii looked her over, stepping around to view her from all sides. Mriy looked much like her mother, except larger and with far more muscle beneath her fur. Watching Seerii as she was inspected was like a mirror into her own future. This is what she would look like in twelve years' time.

"Still fighting shape," Seerii said while she stood behind Mriy. "Carrying human guns hasn't softened you—much."

Mriy jerked her head toward the hunters' kill. "Stronger than that bear you brought. Strong enough to protect the clan."

"So that's the trick," Seerii said. "You want the guardian's job again. That title sat poorly on you last time. No sooner had you won it but you betrayed the clan."

"Soora spat at me," Mriy snapped. "He lost; the job was mine. My blood was still hot and he spat at me. My moment of triumph, and he spat on it. If he was half the fighter he claimed to be, he should have known to defend himself if he was going to do that."

Seerii turned away, but her claws were extended. "You broke most of his ribs and his right arm in three places—all fair, of course. But spitting was all that was left in him. I'm amazed he managed in his condition."

"You talk like he did nothing wrong," Mriy replied. She grabbed Seerii by the shoulder and turned her mother to face her. Five of the hunters flinched toward them, prepared to intervene, but Seerii cut them off with a raised hand. Mriy put her face right in her mother's, looking down the head's height difference between them. "You talk like I deserved to be spat on."

Seerii jerked her shoulder free of Mriy's loose hold. She was still an old woman, so Mriy hadn't dug in her claws. "You'd have made a poor guardian then, and you'd make a worse one now. For two years, you'd spent more time away than home—no harm in that alone. You'd fought and won, but what about the prize money? We didn't send you off-world to fill your hands with gold. You were out there to support the clan."

"I sent back plenty," Mriy replied, flashing her teeth without meaning to. They had always overestimated the winnings from the Silver League.

"Not enough," Seerii countered. "Not enough for how much you were gone. You squandered your time and the clan's money."

Mriy turned her back on her mother, and a pair of younger clan members scrambled to remove themselves from her line of sight. "Same river; new water. I'm here because I brought back Hrykii. A life for a life. Talk of now."

Hrykii spoke up. His voice had deepened in the year since Mriy had last heard him. "So you claim. How do we know it wasn't *you* who kidnapped me? The hero's shadow is the easiest villain."

Mriy grinned. Seerii was being dense, but Hrykii had put rock to steel and made a spark. She slid the data crystal from her pocket, knowing that all eyes in the room followed her movements. "Come to the viewing room. I have proof."

❁ ❁ ❁

Esper laced up the rented shoes and wondered how many wizards' feet had been inside them before hers. They were garishly striped, smooth-soled, and didn't fit perfectly. Who would think of such a bizarre ritual? "Why can't we just bring our own shoes?" she asked.

Mort had changed into his bowling shoes already and was selecting a ball from the racks. "Tradition. Golfers wear plaid knickers, polo players ride live horses, and bowlers wear rented shoes."

The rack was as daunting as it was confusing. Every ball looked a hair different from the others, but identical in all the ways that probably mattered. She picked one at random and was shocked at the weight. "We're going to be throwing these around all afternoon? This thing weighs a ton."

"Sixteen pounds," Mort replied, waving his own in one hand. He had three fingers jabbed into matching holes in the surface. Esper did likewise, but found the spacing uncomfortable.

"What's that in kilos?" she asked.

"It isn't," Mort said. He plucked the ball from her hands, browsed the rack, and handed her another. This one fit her fingers more readily. "Pounds are weight; kilos are mass. Gravity is the difference. Any respectable bowling alley uses Earth gravity. Since this planet is identical, that's a non-issue. But you'll do better if you don't tie your mind up in knots with numbers."

"Why am I doing this to myself?" Esper muttered. The priest was half-baked. She had a mind to report him to the Vatican. Though she had never stopped to consider it before, the Seal of the Confessional probably worked both ways. Whatever cardinal oversaw Meyang likely wouldn't even listen to her grievance.

"Because you said you wanted to keep your magic under control," Mort replied. "And because I am a kindly old wizard, I agreed to help you. This is the place to learn." He took a short, measured walk to the line and rolled his ball down the lane, knocking over every pin.

"I can't compete with your magic," Esper said with a huff. She'd never bowled in her life, and Mort was an experienced wizard, capable of magicking the ball to anywhere in the lane he liked—hers too.

Mort clucked his tongue and wagged a finger. "Not today. Today is all about you. Anything you can to do my ball or yours, do it. I won't try to stop you."

"But you just—"

"Bowled a legitimate strike," Mort finished for her. The primitive mechanics at the end of the lane set up a new rack of ten pins. "I don't need magic to hit a bunch of plastic pins with a ball. You figure out some magic today and you can make me miss, but if you don't, I'm going to mop the floor with you."

Esper mimicked Mort's approach to the line, but skidded to a halt before she was ready to roll. Recovering her balance, she crouched low, set the ball on the floor, and gave it a push. Sixteen pounds of polyurethane wobbled down the lane at the pace of a baby's first steps. Two thirds of the way down, it slipped into the gutter.

Moments later, her ball rolled back to the head of the lane along a pair of polished steel rails. Mort picked it up and brought it back to her. "Practice ball," he said. "This time, tell it where to go. Gesture at it. Use body language. Technique only matters if your opponent can stop you from using magic. Push it with your foot if you want. Just steer it."

Esper gave Mort a wary look as she stepped past him to the line. She took a deep breath, set the ball on the floor, and shoved it with both hands. It took off down the lane, and she could see already that it was heading for the right gutter once more. "Left. Come on, left," she coaxed it, waving a hand for emphasis.

"There you go," Mort said. "Keep at it. Try Latin. The older the language, the better."

"*Sinister. Sin-is-ter... SINISTER!*"

The ball was turning as she waved it over. Esper leapt to her feet, swinging both arms as she cajoled the ball toward the pins. It was hanging on the edge of the gutter. She was almost out of time.

It clipped the rightmost pin. "Yes!" she shouted, clenching a fist in the air.

Quickly she glanced around the alley. There were just four lanes, and only theirs was in use. The attendant ignored her outburst, and the young azrin at the snack counter gave her a thumbs up. Esper offered a self-conscious smile in return.

"Sorry," she whispered to Mort as she got out of his way for the next round.

"Sorry schmorry," Mort replied. "It's a game. Have fun with it. Now let's see what you can do to *my* shot."

❀ ❀ ❀

The viewing room had been upgraded while Mriy had been away. The azrin-made Ruaka Pik holo-projector had been replaced with an authentic Reali-Sim 2655. The holographic field filled half the chamber, and there was no graininess to spoil the illusion of real ships flying overhead. It was odd seeing the *Mobius* from the outside, as the sensor replay simulated the encounter from a third person perspective. There were occasions where bits of debris from the scrapyard faded from view or appeared suddenly as the ship's sensors picked up and lost track of them. Other than that, Mriy and her clan saw the battle just as it had taken place.

"Look at her," Yariy remarked. "If Mriy was at those guns, I wouldn't trust her with a thrown knife. How many shots has she missed?"

"Hrykii was inside," Mriy reminded everyone. "The idea was to maim the ship, not destroy it."

"Better to die than be kept as a trophy, or as a thing to torment," Yariy said. "What if that ship had gotten away?"

"Keep watching," Mriy snapped. Though watching it herself, she had to admit that her aim was wider of the mark than she had remembered.

The critical moment was coming up. The bounty hunter's ship slowed and swung its tail end around. A small object, barely more than a sliver in the holo-field, drifted off in the direction of the *Remembrance*'s momentum as the bounty hunter changed course.

"You can come after me or it, but it's headed for the munitions dump." Mriy glanced around the room, wondering how many of her clan understood human well enough to follow the conversation. They didn't have the benefit of a translator-charmed earring like hers.

The turret gun of the *Mobius* flashed, and this time the shot was a direct hit. The *Remembrance*'s oxygen burned off into space in a fraction of a second.

"We were all set, Mriy. He dropped the pod and was making a run for it," Carl's recorded voice said.

"I know," recorded Mriy replied. *"That was personal."* She wondered if Carl had even noticed that she had stopped speaking his language and swapped back to her native tongue. Wearing a translator charm of his own, Carl would have heard her in his own language either way.

"What did he say?" Seerii asked. "I heard one of them speak your name." Her mother understood human, but Carl wasn't the clearest speaker.

Yariy provided a somber translation. There was a grudging respect in it. Hard to argue when Mriy had disobeyed an order to enact vengeance for the clan.

The holovid continued to the point where the cryostasis pod was secured inside the ship. There were no sensor logs of what took place within. Carl would have been furious to know she had even made a recording of what had gone on outside.

Hrykii stood. "I thank you for my life." He gave a stiff nod and reclaimed his seat.

J.S. Morin

A quiet followed. Eyes turned toward Seerii, awaiting a decision. "How certain are we that this is authentic?" her mother asked Yariy. Mriy's fur bristled at the implication.

The guardian of the Yrris Clan narrowed her eyes. "It's possible she rigged it. We'd need a specialist to analyze it." The implication was clear. Specialist meant human, or possibly laaku. Even Yariy didn't trust her fellow azrins to out-puzzle an ARGO tech specialist. The universities, the ARGO navies, all the best training grounds for tech wranglers were off limits to her people.

"No," Seerii said. "We have Hrykii back. We have this recording. We will not bring this in front of the humans, even paid ones. Mriy destroyed one of their kind. The occupiers would pay more for this as evidence than the clan could afford to pay to keep a human quiet. Your exile is ended, Mriy. You are welcome here once more." She stood and opened her arms.

There were murmurs of quiet conversation around the viewing room, not all of them sounding friendly. But Mriy ignored them and stepped into her mother's embrace, nuzzling against the fur of her neck. How loose the skin there; how slack the sinew. Her mother was old indeed.

"Thank you," Mriy whispered. "I will keep the clan well when my time comes."

Seerii stiffened. She pushed Mriy away firmly, though Mriy did not dare resist for fear of hurting her. "No, you will not take over the clan when I pass. Hrykii is the heir. He was given the title when you were exiled, and it has not been taken from him."

Mriy drew a deep breath. She wanted to scream, to roar, to shake her mother until her senses returned. What good was returning to the Yrris clanhold as neither guardian nor heir? She had not come back to slink into the rank and file of the cousins and mates. She had been second heir after Soora, and Soora was dead.

"Then I challenge, Hrykii, and he will take no shame in backing down," Mriy replied.

"Hah!" Hrykii shouted. "You think you can pay me life for my father's then bargain it away again for leadership of the clan after grandmother? You dragged me here half dead, but we paid a human doctor's ransom. I'll be myself in a day or two."

Mriy gave a soft, hissing laugh. "I could give you two days to heal plus two years to grow muscle on those skinny arms of yours. The day you step into the pit with me, we find you another human doctor."

Several of the Yrris Clan cousins stood and flexed their claws, taking a stand beside Hrykii. But Hrykii smiled. "You could. No doubt, you are a brute. My father learned too late. But since you challenged me, I set the contest. It's my right as heir. I choose the pack hunt."

Mriy's ears flattened. "Getting the clan to do your work for you? Coward."

"My father taught me that the clan isn't about the one, it's about the all. Leading is more than being strongest. Packs of five, in three days' time. See who will follow *you*, brother-killer." Hrykii strode from the room, taking most of the clan with him, including Yariy. She would have been a long shot to join Mriy's pack for the hunt, but sometimes picking the winner is more important than picking the friend.

A minute later, Mriy was alone in the viewing room with Seerii. "It is possible that you might find no one to follow you. If you are alone against a pack of five, maybe you will learn that friends are earned, not won." With that, Seerii left as well.

Seerii's words proved prophetic. Two days scouring the clanhold and making calls on her datapad, and she had a pack of one—herself. Simkin had already agreed to join Hrykii. Tamrau was planning to. Mriy hadn't bothered to ask Yariy. Renyau told her flatly that he hoped she would lose. A dozen weaker hunters had made excuses, avoided speaking with her, or chosen sides against her. Even when she began asking outside the clan, her old acquaintances wanted no part of the hunt.

It was a hard thing to stomach, taking the tally of allies and coming up empty. For a ritual hunt, there could be no payment, no exchange of favors. Mriy had to find hunters who were loyal to her, who wanted to see her win badly enough to spend days in the remote wilderness helping secure her victory. Mriy just didn't have those sorts of friends, it seemed.

Mriy had never found much use for the chapel when she was younger. Years had changed her, not to mention the constant exposure to Esper of late. The Yrris chaplain was still Auzuma, black as the night sky and thin as the crescent moon. He greeted her at the door, as if he had expected her visit.

"Come in Mriy," Auzuma said, his voice smooth and soothing. Auzuma wasn't Yrris; she didn't know how he came into the clan's service. He had been a friend of her father's; that much she knew. The old azrin put a hand on her back and guided her inside the chapel.

Mriy bristled at the touch. As a fighter, she had instincts to suppress any time someone put a friendly hand on her. Caught unawares, she might have broken Auzuma's arm before she could stop herself. Maybe he felt her stiffen. Maybe her ears twitched back. But he let Mriy alone just after she cleared the doorway.

The insides of the chapel smelled of cut evergreen boughs. The pine and spruce resins made the chapel smell like an entire forest had been compressed inside. Mriy took a long breath and let the tension ease out of her—though much of it clung stubbornly.

"I need advice, Father," Mriy said. She sat on a floor cushion in one of the cubbies along the wall, just large enough for two.

"I get few visitors who don't," Auzuma replied, taking a seat beside her. He must have been approaching thirty, but he still moved like a young man. He stretched, and she heard the crackling in his spine as he settled in, spoiling the illusion of youthful vigor.

"Mother has allowed me back home," Mriy began. It was obvious, of course, but it was a hard enough subject even with proper preamble. She couldn't just blurt it out. "But Hrykii is heir. I've challenged him, and he chose the pack hunt."

"Wise of him," Auzuma said, nodding. "A promising sign in a young heir."

"But I can't gather a pack."

"The Mriy I remember was always willing to take on a challenge," Auzuma said. "Would not winning a hunt, alone against five, prove your worth beyond doubt?"

Mriy growled. "No! It would prove me for guardian maybe, but not heir. I could snap Yariy's neck and take the guardian's job any day."

"Then step back," Auzuma said. "Become humble. Show respect for your mother's decision. Ask to be named heir after Hrykii and guard his life more dearly than your own. That would show respect for Seerii and for the good of the clan."

"If I show I can gather a pack, I can prove to mother than I am worthy of being heir, even if not more worthy than Hrykii,"

Mriy said. "I have to show mother that I should never have had my position taken from me."

Auzuma sighed and stood. "Redemption is a powerful motive, and one I can approve. If you will have an old man, I will join your pack for the hunt. No one who comes to the chapel begging aid is turned away without it. If you lose, you will not be shamed by losing alone."

"Thank you, Father Auzuma," Mriy replied, bowing her head.

"But you will want three more," Auzuma said. "I'm too old to be much use. It will take all my strength just to keep up. There are charitable hunters who may take pity on you, but I suggest you set a wider snare. You would not have come to me before looking all the likely places. Time to look in the unlikely ones for hunters."

It was, according to the local omni, the best azrin restaurant for off-worlders in Rikk Pa. The sign outside was lettered in a jumble of azrin script in red chromaglow, but everyone called it by the English translation: Fleshfire. It would have been an unappealing name on a more civilized world, but on Meyang, it carried the comforting connotation of cooked meat, as opposed to the local preference for raw.

The restaurant was a quarter kilometer outside Humantown, and was fancy enough that Esper made sure to shower and change out of her sweaty clothes from bowling. She hadn't come close to catching Mort in any of the eight games they played, but by the end, she was at least rolling the ball with proper form, and adjusting the aim on her throws by a few centimeters. Mort's sure, heavy rolls moved too quickly for her to exert any noticeable influence.

Everyone but Kubu had been invited. He looked so sad when they said goodbye to him at the cargo ramp, but he didn't try to follow. He really was trying to be a good boy. Whether he would ever be accepted into restaurants or any other place of business remained to be seen. For now, he was a rowdy child and far too big a risk to bring along. Not to mention the fact that he looked like a house pet, and it took magic to understand him.

Their booth was in a quiet corner. Whether Carl had said something on the sly to the host or whether Mriy had arranged it in advance was anyone's guess. The dining hall flickered with torchlight. It wasn't the false effect created by software-controlled diodes or even magic, but actual burning wood-and-pitch torches, changed by the waitstaff at regular intervals. A hearty ventilation system sucked the smoke up through the central chimney before it choked the diners.

"Place has some atmosphere," Mort said as he slid into the booth.

Roddy snorted. "Just hope they know how to cook meat. I've seen enough of Mriy's dinners not to want mine raw."

"Hey, according to DinnerBlab, this place is the real deal," Carl said. He took an end seat and slouched down, letting a hand dangle toward the floor.

Mriy was not long behind them, arriving before they had even finished sorting themselves into the booth. "Good. Glad you all made it. I was worried you might have spread over half Meyang by now."

"Nothing personal," Tanny said. "But Meyang isn't exactly bubbling over with tourist spots."

Mriy shook her head. "No time for that now. I have a favor to ask. A big one."

Carl sighed and let his head loll back. "Can't keep cutting you out of future jobs, Mriy."

"Good," Mriy replied. "Because I'm not allowed to pay you for this favor. Not in any way."

"This is sounding promising," Roddy said evenly. "I love not making money. We're getting to be fucking experts at it."

"Hrykii wants a pack hunt, his pack of five against mine," Mriy said. "Win, and I become heir to the clan again. I would take over when my mother passes. But to win, I need a hunting pack."

"That's nice," Esper said. It was like listening to her older brothers talking about sports. What else was there to say? "But what do any of us know about hunting?"

Carl held up his hands and gave a magnanimous smile. "You provide me a Typhoon, and I'll hunt you anything from squirrels all the way up to local patrol ships."

Tanny cuffed him in the shoulder, reaching over Roddy to get at him. "I've had survival training, for what it's worth."

"Much," Mriy replied, nodding. "I was counting on your help. I was also thinking of enlisting Kubu, since he has such an excellent nose."

"Does Kubu know how to track?" Esper asked, not directing the question to anyone in particular.

Tanny laughed out loud, drawing attention from the nearby tables. She tossed a datapad on the table. "Sorry, just struck me. I heard back from that professor today, the one who was going to figure out what Kubu is."

Mriy picked up the datapad first, her expression unreadable as her eyes flicked back and forth. "Blessed God," she whispered. Her eyes went vacant and she stared off in the direction of the *Mobius*, as if it could be seen through the walls of the restaurant.

Roddy snatched the datapad from her hands and began perusing it himself.

"What's it say?" Esper asked.

"Holy hell," Roddy muttered. "Dog's put on twenty kilos since we got him, and this says he hasn't hit a growth spurt yet. He's looking at two or three *tons* by the time he's full grown. By then, he could take that robotic bull over at Human Joe's and use it as a chew toy. His world's got megafauna, and his kind *eats* them."

"So that's a 'yes' on the hunting, I take it?" Esper asked.

Roddy pushed the datapad in Esper's direction. "Let's just say I'm gonna be a lot nicer to that mutt starting now."

"Will they let you bring a dog?" Mort asked.

Mriy shook her head. "No dogs, but I can convince them he's sentient. That will make him a willing pack member, not an animal."

"So, with me and Kubu, you'll have three," Tanny said.

"Four," Mriy corrected her. "My clan's chaplain is part of my pack. His name is Auzuma." Mriy grinned, showing teeth. "Since Hyrkii's pack includes a smoke seer, I have no reservation about bringing a wizard of my own. I would be honored if you would be our fifth, Mort."

Mort leaned back and crossed his arms. "Nope."

"What?" Mriy gasped.

"Feels too much like cheating," Mort replied. "I don't mind the stuff we do, generally. But this is family. I won't be a party to that sort of thing. Besides, it's like I'd be doing all the work for you."

"The prey wears a charm, an heirloom of my clan," Mriy said. "It can't be tracked by magic or science. It has to be hunted by guile and senses."

"Magic's magic," Mort replied. "You think your local witchdoctors are going to fool *me*? I'm sure that charm can discombobulate scientific whosamajiggers, but you're daft if you think I couldn't sniff that charm out from miles away if I was of a mind."

Mriy sank back in her seat. "Auzuma may know a protective charm or two, but I could use a proper wizard."

"Take Esper," Mort replied. "I spent all day giving her a rundown of the basics."

"Esper?" Mriy asked, confusion clear in her tone.

"Esper?" Esper asked, clearly not having heard correctly. She was no wizard. She knew one spell and knew it badly enough that she'd accidentally killed someone with it when it was supposed to heal.

Mort shrugged. "You're young. Got healthy lungs in you. Getting away from science for a few days'll do you some good. Practice away from the heavy expectations of civilization. Magic's harder where people rely on techno-gizmos. Breathe some fresh air, levitate twigs, make the birds fly funny."

"I need a wizard, not..." Mriy struggled for a word and settled for gesturing to Esper.

"Me."

"You," Mriy confirmed.

Esper looked down at the menu in front of her, but the words didn't register. They were English, but her mind was on Mriy's opinion of her, not the food selection. She just couldn't look the azrin in the eye.

"Don't even *think* about looking at me," Roddy said, breaking the awkward silence. "A few days without booze or tech, I'd be ready to fucking kill myself."

Carl looked off into the restaurant, for all indications taking in the ambiance. "You know, there's more to being a leader than picking a bunch of ringers. Sometimes, pack leader—or a captain—might just have to take the ones she's got because they're the only ones who'll have her. Esper's no wizard like Mort, but who the hell is? She's a quick learner, and she'd be better use in the woods than I'd be. I couldn't sneak up on a cow unless it was in a bun with ketchup and bacon."

"We will hunt an elk, not cow," Mriy said.

"Point is," Carl said. "I'd suggest you ask Esper nicely, else you might be running with a pack of four. I'm guessing we were your last stop."

Mriy was silent. Esper listened, and all she heard was breathing and the rustling of clothes as the *Mobius* crew shifted uneasily in that silence. She spared a glance up and saw that Mriy was staring at her. The azrin had been waiting to make eye contact. "Will you help me?" Mriy asked.

There were a dozen reasons to refuse. Mriy obviously hadn't wanted her along. Mriy didn't think she would be any use, and who could blame her. Esper didn't know anything about hunting and had never eaten anything she'd killed herself. She'd even gone through a phase where she didn't eat meat. The seminary had taught her that animals were God's gift to mankind, meant to be eaten, used to carry burdens, or kept as pets. This wasn't wanton sport; it was a time-honored azrin ritual, and she had no place mucking it up. And as much as she hated to admit it, she liked datapads and holovids, food processors and voice-activated environmental controls. The woods had none of that.

But Mriy needed her. She hadn't asked because Esper was any good. Mriy needed her because she was all she had. How could Esper refuse? "I'll help you."

Hopefully there would be enough time before the hunt to look a few things up on the omni, starting with "how to hunt."

The *Mobius* lifted off as soon as Auzuma was aboard. Tanny hadn't waited another minute before she got them out of the Yrris Clanhold. The *Yinnak* had a minute's head start en route to the hunting grounds, and hadn't left them any coordinates. She had no idea what the azrin custom was for forfeiture or concession in regard to tardiness or never finding the hunting grounds, but she'd be damned if it was going to be her fault that they lost track of the clan's ship.

Tanny had been to Earth-like worlds before. The similarities had always comforted her—familiar geography, familiar climate, familiar gravity. But Meyang was a bit spartan. It was like someone had taken Earth and stripped away civilization. Cities were pockets of modern life amid primordial forests and trackless seas. The hotbeds of culture and the population centers so common on Earth-like worlds were barren. The *Yinnak* took an erratic course, wandering the planet from the upper atmosphere.

"Are they giving us a tour, or are they just lost?" Carl wondered aloud. He stood behind the copilot's seat, leaning his forearms on the headrest.

"Maybe they're trying to keep us guessing," Tanny ventured. "Jesus, this place is empty. It's like someone turned a natural history museum inside out, and they've got a planet full of people stuffed in an old building somewhere."

"Weird seeing the British Isles uninhabited," Carl said. "We ever look at the population survey?"

"Less than forty million," Tanny replied. "They can afford to pick and choose."

The *Yinnak* sped over Africa and across the southern Atlantic—or at least Meyang's equivalents. They crossed into South America and followed the Andes Mountain range north. The greens were so green, the blues so blue. Earth and Phabian, pillars of ARGO, were monuments of silver and glass, inhabited to the point of bursting. Meyang was an arboreal world, ripe for lumbering. Even the moon above was a pale white rock, with no sign of cities or orbital traffic.

It was in the northern part of Meyang's Rocky Mountain analogue that the Yinnik finally landed. Tanny set the *Mobius* down a hundred meters away.

"You take it easy with this thing while I'm gone," Tanny said, giving Carl a stern glare. "No racing, no daredevil bullshit, nothing that'll get the *Mobius* impounded."

Carl held up his hand for a courtroom oath. "I will be a model citizen." The smirk didn't make him convincing.

She cringed as he slipped into the pilot's chair before she'd even left the cockpit. He wriggled into position, as if trying to form the seat to his backside.

"Not even going to wish us luck?" she asked.

"Since when have I ever been good luck to anyone?"

Tanny thought a moment. "Fair enough."

"Just keep them as safe as you can," Carl replied. "This isn't a fight, it's a hunt. Worst thing if Mriy loses is she gets written out of her mother's will, or however the hell that works around here. Not worth anyone getting hurt over."

Tanny shouldered the knapsack with her survival supplies. "Tell that to the Yrris Clan."

The rest of the hunting pack was waiting for her in the cargo bay, with Mort and Roddy there to see them off. It was a motley bunch. Mriy was the only one who looked like a proper hunter. Auzuma was an old man, though Mriy had told her that he was a year younger than her thirty-one years. Tanny wasn't quite sure how to take that, but it made her glad she was human. For all the times that she'd occasionally envied

Mriy's easy strength and feline reflexes, she'd outlive the azrin by decades. Esper looked like she'd packed for a holiday camping trip, all store-bought new. It was going to be a chore just getting her to contribute, let alone be an asset. Kubu was the only one who looked excited.

"It is time to go now?" Kubu asked. "Kubu wants to go hunting."

Tanny eyed the canine—or *canis ultra poltidae* as scientists had dubbed his species. "Extreme dog from Poltid" was the translation. Was he bigger than yesterday? She needed to start scanning him more often.

"Yes and no," Tanny answered. "Yes, we're going outside now, and that's where we'll be hunting. But hunting is going to take a long time. We won't find what we're looking for right away."

"You can really understand that beast?" Auzuma asked, eyeing Kubu. The old azrin and Kubu had fur the same shade of black, but could not have looked more distinct otherwise. Auzuma was tall and wiry, and moved with a statesman's grace. Kubu was a barrel with legs and jaws that boiled with eager energy.

"Same as I understand you," Tanny replied, flicking her earring. Auzuma understood English just fine, thankfully. Mort wasn't going to provide another translator charm just so the azrin could understand Kubu. "Mort and Roddy understand your language, but they're not part of the hunt."

Roddy reached up and slapped the button that started lowering the cargo bay door. "May the wind blow your way," he said. Some funny cadence in the words suggested to Tanny that she was hearing the translator charm's interpretation of Roddy's azrin. Showoff little smartass.

The wind was indeed blowing as Mriy and her pack exited the *Mobius*, but it wasn't blowing any way Tanny wanted to claim as her own. If Rikk Pa had been cold, this area was frigid. On Earth, they'd have been a few hours walk outside Calgary Prime. She didn't know what it was called on Meyang, but she had a few colorfully vulgar suggestions.

The *Yinnak*'s passengers were disembarking as well, none so bundled against the cold as Tanny and Esper were. The azrin wore heavy vests and leggings, but still left much of their fur exposed. Kubu wore nothing and didn't show the first sign of being bothered by the weather. His breath came in steaming bellows as his tongue lolled and he bounced on front and hind legs like a bucking horse.

"There is our prey," Mriy said, pointing. The Yrris Clan was unloading a beast from their ship. Tanny was no expert on tundra wildlife, but Mriy had informed them that they should be hunting elk. It was as tall at the shoulder as its azrin handlers, with a rack of antlers that rose to twice that height. Unless the local fauna had taken a drastic twist from Earth's, its green and orange coloration was painted on.

"What're those symbols?" Esper asked, saving Tanny the trouble of looking the fool for not knowing.

"It marks our prey," Auzuma answered. "No azrin will interfere with the challenge by killing it. The medallion around its neck conceals it from science and magic alike. It is for us to find and kill, no others."

"We hunt that?" Kubu asked. He took off at once, accelerating to a full run in three strides, sending up a wake in hip-deep snow that seemed to do little to slow him.

"Kubu, stop!" Mort shouted. They all turned to see the wizard following them. Kubu skidded to a halt in a self-made snowdrift. "Not now. They'll tell you when it's time."

"Mort, what are you doing out here?" Tanny called out.

The wizard trudged through the snow in sneakers and jeans. His only concession to the cold was keeping his hands in the front pocket of his hooded sweatshirt. "Decided I'm going to keep an eye on things. Mriy's clan might play things on the level; they might not. With me around, they won't dare slant things Hrykii's way."

Mriy's ears flattened back. "I don't think my mother will approve."

"Then I'll just point out that we're a long way from things out here," Mort replied. "And there's more than one way to inherit a clanhold."

"You will not threaten—"

"I won't have to," Mort snapped. "I *am* a threat. You've gotten used to having a wizard around, but most azrin haven't. They're sensible, superstitious folk—smart enough to take heed of a wizard. They'll worry about me wilting their crops or sickening their herds, when they should really be wondering whether I'd incinerate them or crush them into a grapefruit-sized ball of meat. But the result's the same. They'll let me oversee."

Mort hung back as they approached the *Yinnak*. There was a brief ceremony where strips of cloth were rubbed against the elk's hide, then passed out to each member of both packs. Tanny tucked hers away without giving it the elaborate sniffing that the azrins did. Her human nose had no use for scent in tracking. Not her job on this expedition.

"Most of you know the rules," Seerii said. "For the outsiders, this is a traditional hunt. No weapons that shoot. Anything that harms the prey must be a part of you or held in hand. The prey will be left in the mountains. None of the hunters know where we will leave it. It will be at least one day's travel from here; beyond that I will not say. The prey must be returned to this spot, dead, for the bearer to be declared winner of the challenge."

Seerii did not ask if anyone had questions, or whether they were unclear on the protocol of the hunt. Tanny had the impression that even the little she said was a concession to Mriy's odd pack. The members of the Yrris Clan loaded the animal back into the *Yinnak*, and Mort followed them. There followed a quiet but heated discussion, and at the conclusion, Mort joined the azrins in the ship.

"We move," Mriy ordered. Hrykii's pack was already starting out, following the general direction of the *Yinnak* as it headed off to the northwest. Kubu bounded to the front of the group, running ahead and circling back to Mriy. He was clearly unfamiliar with the concept of conserving strength. Tanny waited until Auzuma and Esper fell into step behind their pack leader, and then took up the rear.

Just then, the engines of the *Mobius* roared to life. It lifted skyward, kicking up a storm of powdery snow that coated Mriy's hunting pack. The ship rolled over so that the landing gear faced deep space and tore across the evergreen forest at treetop height, threatening to topple the ancient pines. In the distance a moment later, the *Mobius* headed straight up, spinning like a corkscrew before taking an orbital trajectory and disappearing from sight.

Tanny's footsteps crunched in the snow, audible with the departure of the two ships and the increasing distance between the members of the pack. She didn't worry about keeping up so much as she did what would become of the ship with just Carl and Roddy looking after it. "Maybe I can work for Mriy after they get it impounded."

Mriy's kinfolk gathered around Mort as if he were a zoo exhibit. He let them look. None approached within arm's reach of him, but they conversed among themselves.

"Why did Seerii agree to this?" one muttered out of the side of his mouth, never taking his eyes from Mort.

"I don't know, but I don't like his look. Could we throw him out the door and be done with him?"

"He's a wizard."

"He's scrawny."

"Still a wizard."

"And can understand every word you're saying," Mort added, speaking in Jiara. This had the effect of splashing cold water on the group. They flinched back and looked at him in shock.

"You speak our language?" one asked. He had a dim look, even if Mort wasn't generally one to judge intra-species facial expressions.

"No, you gigantic floor mop," Mort replied. "I'm just speaking random words and got lucky."

"What did you call me?" the floor mop demanded.

Mort held up a placating hand. "Perhaps the comparison was out of line. But you're a horse's ass for talking about me like you just were. I'm here to keep this contest on the straight and narrow. No funny business. No sticking our noses in. Just let the chips fall where they may."

"I think he was telling the truth about guessing," one of the smaller azrin said. "Those are all words, but they make no sense."

Mort seethed out a long breath. Idioms might as well have been riddles. "Idiots, I am here to make certain the contest is fair." He spoke slowly, as if they were new at understanding their own language.

"Wasting your time, then," an orange-furred Yrris said. "No fair contest between Mriy's pathetic pack and Hrykii's hunters."

"Ignoring that," Mort said. "I want no interference. We drop this beast off, then go back and wait for them to bring it."

"We didn't bring human food."

"Shit," Mort muttered, remembering to use English. He had no reason to insult their food, though in truth the whole planet's cuisine could use a good insult or two. A whole species had managed to have an industrial revolution without inventing baking, sausage, or soup. Spices had been introduced by human conquerors. "I don't suppose you lot can order take-out wherever we are?"

❁ ❁ ❁

Roddy vaulted over the armrest and into the copilot's chair. "What's the plan, Captain?"

Carl smirked. It wasn't often that Roddy got all naval with titles. "Haven't decided yet. Plan on enjoying a little flying though, while I've got the ship to myself—present company excepted, of course. Meyang's not really my cup of tea."

"Yeah," Roddy agreed. He slouched down in the seat and reached for the console with one of his feet. He turned the volume on the sound system down to a whisper. "Listen, I got a thing."

"A thing?"

"You know, an idea," Roddy replied. "For you."

"Just spit it out." Carl started to wonder what sort of plans Roddy was hinting at.

"You know that sword? The magic one we all keep telling you you're going to kill yourself with?" Roddy asked.

Of course, Carl knew it. It had set him back 4,000 credits and had seemed like a bargain at the time. It was sharp enough to slice steel like a ripe tomato and weighed next to nothing. "What about it?"

Roddy tossed Carl a datapad. "They've got this guy, a local. Real whiz with weapons. Ancient azrin techniques and all that shit. He's the only one teaching these secrets to off-worlders."

Carl glanced over the advert for Master Yuuwai Viyaa. It was flashy and slick, the sort of thing that Martian ad agencies cranked out for borderlands companies, where the locals weren't as sophisticated as back in Sol. "Sounds like a scam." People of every race and species had been pulling stunts like that for as long as explorers had been discovering new lands. Some rich bastards plunked themselves down on your land, and if you couldn't fight them off, you soaked them for every terra they had.

"You're signed up starting tomorrow, dawn local time," Roddy said.

"What?" Carl scowled at the laaku mechanic, searching that simian face for any sign that he was joking. But if there was one thing Roddy was awful at, it was keeping a straight face while making a joke. With his dead calm, he could have been at a funeral.

"My dime," Roddy replied. "You don't like it, bail after the first day. But it's on a tropical island, and you might come back a badass swordsman. So you might think twice before spending however-the-fuck long that hunt goes joyriding."

"What's the catch?" Carl asked. "You've got an angle."

"I'm lazy," Roddy admitted. "You with a few days behind the yoke on this baby, I might never be done putting it right. I'd be overhauling every maneuvering thruster, replacing coolant lines, and patching up stress cracks in the hull for months. It's worth a few hundred terras out of my own pocket to ground you."

"I could say 'no,'" Carl suggested, probing for a reaction.

"Badass. Swordsman. Tropical. Island. The Earth name for the island is Fiji, by the way."

"Fucker," Carl muttered. "What time is it there now?"

Roddy took back his datapad and checked the built-in chrono. "4:33 AM. You're gonna want to get a move on."

"Get a move on," Tanny shouted.

Esper had lagged behind the rest of the pack, and Tanny had slowed to stay behind her. Her knapsack was heavier than it had been earlier in the day, despite containing one less meal and a liter or so less water. The snow was harder to force her feet through, even though it wasn't as deep.

"I'm trying," she replied, not caring whether Tanny could hear. Esper couldn't spare enough breath to shout back. Dusk had come and gone, and a clear sky with a bright half moon was the only reason they could see ahead.

The stars poked out through the darkened atmosphere, taunting. *You could fly if you were on a ship*, they whispered down to her. *You've barely gone twenty kilometers.* Esper knew she was imagining it, that it was her own voice she was hearing. That didn't make her any less cross with the stars.

Tanny's steps drew closer, their pace quicker. A hand reached out and unclasped the buckle that secured Esper's knapsack around her waist. "Hey, what—"

"No time for this," Tanny muttered as she slipped the knapsack off Esper's back and slung it over her shoulder. It was an awkward fit with Tanny's already in place, but the ex-marine managed. "Hrykii's pack is probably five klicks ahead of us by now."

"Sorry."

Tanny shook her head. "It's not just you. Auzuma's not doing much better. We're going to have to stop soon for camp, even if we lose ground in the night."

"You think they'll push through?" Esper asked.

"No idea. But I bet they could if they wanted to. Look at Mriy. She'd be good to go all night. Kubu, too." The canine's energy was inexhaustible out in the cold. He puffed and panted, breath fogging the air like an old-timey steam locomotive. But he kept going without complaint. In fact, it was the happiest she'd seen him.

If nothing else, the scenery was spectacular. When Esper wasn't watching where her feet were landing, trying to follow the trodden snow where Mriy and Auzuma had passed, the mountains loomed majestically around them. She had to look away and ignore them for a while for them to ever appear any larger. Watching them the whole while, they never seemed to grow or come any closer.

Night had settled in fully by the time Mriy agreed to call a halt. The pack had been following a creek for the last few hours and settled into a bend where it wound around one of the foothills. Their campsite had them sheltered from the direction of the wind. Esper had lost track of the compass direction when the sun had finished setting, so she didn't know quite which way that was. But it was welcome having some protection from air that cut through the gaps between her hat and scarf to rob her body of heat.

"Auzuma, Esper, set up camp," Mriy said, dropping her load of supplies in the snow. "Tanny, Kubu, let's patrol the area to make sure we're alone out here." There was an unfamiliar hardness in her words. Mriy hadn't done much commanding on the *Mobius*. Carl was in charge—to a degree. Tanny did most of their tactical work on the ground. Everyone listened to Mort. Roddy obeyed orders when he chose. Mriy mostly went along, at least as long as Esper had known her. If she ever expressed a preference, it was for expediency, not for getting a job done right.

The old azrin stepped beside her and they watched side by side as the patrol departed over their sheltering hill. "Have you set up a camp before?" Auzuma asked.

"No," Esper admitted.

"You don't belong out here, do you?"

"No."

"Then I give my deepest thanks," Auzuma said. Esper gave him a furrowed glare. If the azrin could read human expressions at all, hers was likely lost under thick-bundled outerwear. "It's an easy thing to help someone when you know how. It is the act of a friend to help when the helping is a burden."

"She didn't want me along," Esper said, hanging her head. "She didn't have many options."

"You came for the same reason I did," Auzuma said. He put a hand on her shoulder, heavy even through three layers of fabric. "You have compassion. It is a trait that runs thick in God's servants."

Esper looked up. "She told you?" The azrin nodded. "I'm not anymore, you know. I ran. If I was any sort of priestess, I'd have gone back and faced the music."

"Music?" Auzuma echoed. He waved aside his own puzzlement as if it was of no consequence. "You left a church. I can tell you haven't left His service."

"You sound more sure of that than I am," Esper replied.

"I must be a better judge of character, then," he said. "I'm no fool. Mriy doesn't deserve our help in this. She was wrong to make her challenge. Hrykii is a fool, too, but he is young and less set in his ways. It is Seerii that Mriy disrespects by this quest for the title of heir."

"Then why did you come?" Esper asked. "I felt pity for Mriy and figured if I didn't help her, no one would. She didn't want me. She might even have been better off without me."

"God's word reached your world, same as it did mine," Auzuma said. "So I know you understand redemption. Mriy is not worthy to win, but by the end of this challenge, perhaps she will be. Now, let's get started putting a camp together."

Cold wind cleared the head. Seerii had taught her that. Mriy had a lot of time on the hike for thinking, but not much for discussing strategy for the hunt. There was little need for a patrol. That might have been a sensible precaution if Hrykii's pack was within an hour's hike of them, but Mriy couldn't imagine that to be the case.

"We need to talk," Mriy said, letting Tanny draw close. The human had kept up well. She hadn't sagged under the pace or the burden of taking on Esper's gear. She was a boon to the pack.

"I figured as much," Tanny replied. "We're up shit's creek, aren't we?"

"The creek's name escapes me," Mriy replied, glancing in the direction of the rushing water, even though the terrain hid it from direct view.

"No, I mean we're not winning this," Tanny clarified. "Those two are slowing us down. Your nephew's going to have the prey back to your mother before we get halfway to them."

Mriy stretched and flexed her back, looking up into the night sky. "Normally the slow pack sets an ambush to steal the prey. I'm worth two of them, and you might hold your own, but that won't be enough."

"You're allowed to fight each other on the hunt?" Tanny asked.

"Of course," Mriy replied. "You heard my mother set out the rules. She said nothing about our conduct. The mountains are vast and quiet. We won't kill them, but leaving them maimed and taking the prey is a valid tactic."

"Might have mentioned that *before* we signed up."

"You would have come anyway," Mriy replied. Tanny didn't shy from fights. Mriy knew she secretly relished combat, which humans found unbecoming.

"Maybe, but not Esper."

"No," Mriy agreed. "And I think it is time to fix my mistakes."

"Send her back? After a full day out here? She's going to be pissed."

"Her and Auzuma. Neither belongs. We are too slow to race Hrykii's pack and too weak to fight them."

Kubu made a curious noise, a whine that rose in pitch. Nothing came in translation, so it was not meant to be any sort of word. He cocked his head and sniffed the air. Mriy sniffed along by reflex, but picked up no scent on the wind.

"Kubu is hungry," Kubu said, using a quiet voice she had rarely heard him employ. He bounded off into the low brush, little more than a thicket of spindly twigs devoid of leaves. He disappeared from sight.

"Kubu!" Tanny shouted, starting off after him. "Kubu, get back here!"

Mriy followed Tanny, but knew that neither of them was going to catch Kubu unless he stopped or doubled back. Azrins were faster than humans in short bursts, but not by nearly the margin that Kubu exhibited. A snarl sounded from the darkness, followed by barking and a ferocious growl. Tanny quickened her pace, rushing headlong and drawing a hunting knife in stride as she ran.

A pained shriek split the night air, followed by more growling. When they caught sight of Kubu, he had a lynx by the neck; the creature dangled limp from either side of his jowls. He shook it like a chew toy, then dropped it in the snow. Wasting no time, he tore into the kill and ripping open the lynx's belly. The carcass steamed in the moonlight.

Mriy had killed with her bare hands before. She had torn out a deer's throat and tasted the warm blood. She had even eaten a hot kill in the wild once or twice, despite the mess and having to eat around the hide and unsavory organs, not to mention bones. But she had never seen a hunter eat like Kubu. His meal started like a wolf's feast, with the easy, the juicy, the nutritious. But he didn't stop there. He didn't strip flesh from bone, didn't tear away the skin and fur. He bit through limb and torso alike, crunching great mouthfuls of anything he could fit between his jaws—which for the lynx, happened to be everything.

It took two minutes, perhaps as long as three. Mriy spared no attention from the spectacle to check a chrono. The lynx was gone. Kubu even gobbled up several mouthfuls of snow that had been spattered with blood, and a few more that hadn't, just for the water.

"How much do you think that thing weighed?" Tanny asked quietly.

Mriy did some quick figuring in human units. "Eight or ten kilos. It wasn't a big one."

Kubu ambled over to them, tongue working around the edges of his muzzle to clean the mess from his face. "Kubu not so hungry now."

Mriy remembered a time, not so long ago at all, when she'd had to wrestle Kubu to the ground. He had gotten into Tanny's chemical supplements, the ones that humans gave to their soldiers to make them strong, fast, and aggressive. She had overwhelmed him with leverage and technique. But she remembered the strength, the corded, sinewy muscle like iron, just below his fur. He was growing by the day. Even now, could she have managed the same feat?

"You sure we can't fight them?" Tanny asked.

"Even if we could, I'm not certain we should," Mriy replied. "I don't see a middle ground between defeat and a distasteful meal. But we're keeping Kubu with us. Lose Esper and Auzuma, and we become the faster pack."

❀ ❀ ❀

By the time the patrol returned, Esper and Auzuma had erected the tents and gathered firewood. The two azrin tents were little more than large, droopy umbrellas with the lone occupant meant to curl around the pole and pull it down until the dome touched ground. Esper and Tanny were to share a traditional human-style camping tent that might have fit Kubu as well. Fortunately, the canine had happily dug himself a hole in the snow and curled up outside.

Esper had chopped some small branches into firewood with a carbon-bladed hatchet and was trying to get the green wood to catch fire. "This is stupid," she muttered. "Why can't we just have a little fire-starter laser? It's not like we could hunt anything with it." She struck the rock against the steel blade of her hunting knife and watched the sparks die on the bark of her branches.

It was Mort's idea for her to come out here. Get away from technology, he'd said. She was supposed to be practicing, learning to control her magic. Learning not to kill people, was more like it. Esper had insisted everyone go through a medical scan before the hunt, to make sure they wouldn't grow anything malignant if she had to use her one reliable spell on them. Speeding the body's natural healing seemed so innocuous—until you considered that cancer was going to thrive as well. What could she do wrong trying a little fire? The possibilities seemed exponentially greater.

Still, it was deathly cold with deeper temperatures to come before morning. "You are on fire," she whispered to the twigs. Nothing happened. "Fire." Nothing happened. She tried to picture the twigs aflame. "Fire." Nothing happened. "*Ignis.*" She thought for a moment that the switch to Latin had done it. But the wisp of smoke had been her imagination. She tried to recall the word Mort had taught her, one of a handful he'd made her memorize before embarking on the hunt.

Remembering another bit of Mort's advice, she stopped trying to remember the word and just spoke it. It lacked form and shape on her lips. She could not have written it down or explained how to pronounce it. Mort had spoken it to her, and it had wormed its way into her head. But the language of angels and demons combined with her imaging of burning twigs turned that wish real. She leapt back, falling onto her backside and hands in the snow as the campfire caught.

"Nice work," Tanny said. "I was never much at starting fires. Glad you figured it out. Find a tutorial on the omni or something?"

"Or something," Esper muttered. From the corner of her eye, she caught Auzuma watching her with interest. Was he smiling?

They ate a quiet meal, all except for Kubu, who slept. They talked about the day's hike and where Hrykii's pack might have ventured. Mriy mentioned the hardships that lay ahead, and Tanny talked about how much ground they were going to have to make up. By the time everyone settled into their tents, Esper had grown suspicious.

Curled up in a sleeping bag, just a few centimeters from Tanny, there was no room for secrets. "You two don't want me here," she said.

Tanny faced away from Esper, not bothering to roll over to address her. "What Mriy and I said was true. How you take it is up to you."

"You don't have Carl's talent for it."

"Huh?"

"For lying," Esper said. "You're as subtle as a sermon. You want me to volunteer to go back, so you don't have to tell me I'm not welcome."

"Mriy hadn't said anything before, but it can get rough out here," Tanny said. "If we don't get to the prey first, we're expected to try to ambush Hrykii's pack to take it from them. People are going to get hurt out here."

"All the more reason you need me," Esper reasoned. After all, healing was the one thing she seemed to have tidied up in her repertoire. "I won't give up."

"Then you'd better keep up tomorrow," Tanny said. "And you'd better get to sleep. You're going to need the energy."

In the end, Mort and the Yrris Clan found a human-food restaurant with a 500-kilometer delivery radius. In an act of magnanimity, he offered to introduce them to one of Earth's most azrin-friendly cuisines. He sat surrounded by azrin in the *Yinnak*'s dining hall, which was smaller than the common room of the *Mobius* and designed for creatures with their feline legs pointing the wrong way. He thought it gave him some insight into the trouble Mriy must have had with human chairs.

"What is this?" Yuanan asked. He had gray-fur was missing the tip of one ear. His coloration was natural, not a sign of age, Mort had learned.

"We call it sashimi," Mort replied. "It's got all sorts of fancy names by the meat inside, but damned if I know most of them. This place had a menu with azrin dishes, light on the vegetable components. Mine's the stuff in the yellow plastic container. The rest is for you fine folks to share."

It had cost a small fortune between feeding a dozen azrin and paying some poor slob to trek it out to them, but Mort was looking for some way to break the ice with Mriy's family. He might be holed up with them for days, so friendly terms were a lifestyle improvement over their cold silence and blank looks.

Frouniy opened the much larger white package and unwrapped several bundles. "Shrimp. Tuna. Some other fish. Is this all ocean food?"

Mort gave Frouniy a nod of confirmation. "There are some specialty dishes that use other meat, but since this is your first time, I'm sticking to the traditional."

"Traditional is good," Yuanan agreed. In the absence of Yariy, he had been acting as guardian. Mort had overheard two of them talking in the next room.

"Before Seerii eats, you eat," Ryhma said, narrowing her eyes and leaning in as if Mort was going to flinch or blanch or make some other damned fool slip-up in the commission of betrayal. It would have been funny if they weren't so deadly serious. Not one of them had an ounce of guile for human deception.

Mort snickered. "I took the precaution of only ordering things I'd eat. Figured you lot might be paranoid." He picked up a tuna roll and popped it into his mouth. It tasted funny with a thin wrapping of beef jerky in place of seaweed, but not a bad sort of funny. Just wasn't what he'd expected. "How many you want me to try?"

"All of them," Yuanan said.

"Fuck that," Mort said. "I got my own to eat, and I'm not a bottomless pit. Use a science thingy to check it, or have one of your own taste the food. You don't trust it, pitch it in the snow."

"You *will* eat it," Yuanan snarled, rising to his feet.

"Listen, Fluffy, if you think you can bully me, give it a go," Mort replied. He reached out and picked up one of his tuna rolls and popped it into his mouth. He chewed as he continued. "But I'm not in the mood for your shit."

"If you were a hunter, you'd have gone with Mriy, if you're so worried about her," Yuanan reasoned. "I think you are a warm wind."

Mort leaned over to Seerii, who had stayed out of the confrontation thus far. "Did he just accuse me of flatulence?"

Seerii shook her head. "He accuses you of talking more than being. He thinks you bluff."

"Oh."

Mort swallowed his tuna roll and stood. Yuanan must have seen something in his unconcerned posture that gave him pause. The azrin cringed back, but held his ground. Mort stepped forward, put a hand on the azrin's chest, and shoved him through the nearest wall. There was no crash, no splatter; Yuanan simply passed through solid steel—or whatever azrins made ships out of. Mort wasn't sure on that front.

"What did you do to him?" Seerii demanded. The other Yrris bystanders scrambled to put distance between themselves and Mort. Warm wind indeed.

"I threw him outside into the snow to cool off," Mort replied. "And Mriy asked me to join her pack, but I refused. Wouldn't have been fair. I could sniff that ox of yours out by the magic—don't tell me I couldn't. Then I could have ridden it back here, killed it at your feet, and been back sleeping in my own bed by nightfall. But I didn't. Wouldn't have been fair. I'm *very* interested in this contest playing out fair."

The azrins watched him in silence. They seemed not to know whether to attack him en masse or offer a surrender, exchanging glances that may have carried more communication than met the (human) eye.

Yuanan burst back into the room, throwing open the door in the process. He was dusted with snow, and his boots were leaving wet prints on the floor as he strode over to Mort, teeth bared. "How dare you—"

Mort didn't move, except to stuff another tuna roll in his mouth. Yuanan reached for him, but found his footing gone from beneath him. Without so much as the shove he'd given the last time, Mort levitated Yuanan and threw him through the wall yet again. Ryhma crept over and pressed a hand against the wall, but it was fully solid.

"I can keep this up all night," Mort replied. "I haven't even broken a sweat." He glanced around the dining hall. Mriy was a tough nut to crack when it came to reading facial expressions.

Her clanmates were not so reserved. Mort found a mix of fear, anger, confusion, and hints of amusement at Yuanan's plight. He held out the white container to Seerii. "Grab some sashimi. I didn't poison the goddamn things. I've killed more people than all of you put together, and I'm long past being shy about it."

Seerii reached a tentative hand and picked up a shrimp roll in two extended claws. "This will be a fair contest."

❀ ❀ ❀

The *Mobius* climbed into orbit at a leisurely pace, leaving the azrins' take on Fiji far below. The crew was gone, off playing savages in the snowy wilderness. Carl was checking into his sword-fighting resort. Roddy had the ship to himself. All he heard were the mechanical sounds of the engines, the life support, the hum of the computer coolant system. It was bliss.

He'd never liked the ship's control layout. It had come as-is and configured for human comfort. The seat was too long and too far back from the yoke, and everything just seemed to be spaced wrong on the panels. It was hard to pin down exactly why, but the ship clearly had not been built with laaku ergonomics in mind. Ignoring the mild annoyances, he keyed the comm for the local ARGO patrol fleet.

"Orbital control, this is Earth-registered vessel *Mobius*. Request long-term orbit."

"*Vessel Mobius, state your reason for orbital clearance.*"

Roddy shrugged, though the comm was voice only. "I've got some maintenance to do, the ship to myself while the crew's planetside, and I just wanted the view."

"*Will your maintenance interfere with your ship ID broadcast, engine signature, or involve deviation from a proscribed orbit?*"

"None of the above," Roddy replied. "Sub-system overhauls and preventative maintenance only."

"You are cleared for long-term orbit. Transmitting a trans-polar orbital path. Enjoy your sightseeing."

"Thank ya kindly," Roddy replied and shut off the comm. "I give those boys too much shit sometimes. This garrison seems pretty laid back." He followed the transmitted heading, then rolled the ship up so the forward windows looked down on Meyang.

By the side of the seat, Roddy found his guitar case. Of late, it had seemed more like Carl owned it—he certainly played it more these days. But it belonged to Roddy, and it was past time to brush the rust off his fingers and play it a little. It was a double-neck, a style invented by humans even though they couldn't play both at once. It was the laaku that had taken the design and made a proper instrument out of it. His guitar had been made on Phabian, in a little factory just outside Kethlet. It was as old a friend as he had.

He strummed both sets of strings and cringed. Carl had an ear for good music, but he was as good as tone deaf when it came to playing it. Roddy spent the next few minutes with an acoustic analyzer, tuning each string to mathematical perfection. Each chord he tried rang beautifully. "There ya go, baby. That's the guitar I know."

He reclined the pilot's chair and slouched back until he could comfortably balance while all four hands played. He picked a human song. He'd grown up on human music, thanks to his old man. It wasn't one that was supposed to have a guitar part, but it was the first thing that came to mind, so he made it work. Before human contact, laaku music hadn't had lyrics except for hymns; it had just seemed sacrosanct to those laaku from way back.

"That's just one damn pretty ball of rock down there," he mused as he played. Phabian had looked like that once, a long, long time ago. There were still a few nature preserves; it wasn't Earth, after all. But the blue-green orb covered in wispy clouds only existed in pictures, in museums, and on the Earth-likes. It grated a little that the term had caught on. They were Phabian-like, to Roddy's thinking.

He strummed with his feet for a moment while he grabbed a beer from a six-pack he'd brought with him to the cockpit. After a long pull and a refreshed gasp, he set back to playing with all four hands, this time singing along with his own accompaniment. He picked up midway through.

"...and I think to myself, what a wonderful world."

❀ ❀ ❀

Whatever Tanny had said to Esper in the night, it had not been to give up and return to the *Yinnak*. Every time Mriy looked over her shoulder, she expected to see the human fallen hopelessly far behind. Each time, she was surprised to find her keeping pace. It was Auzuma that was the trouble. He was lagging, and Mriy didn't know how to get rid of him in any way that would save face.

Auzuma had been with the Yrris Clan since before she was born. He might outlive Seerii, if their relative health was any measure. How could Mriy win back the title of heir, then take over the clan while Auzuma was still chaplain? He would oversee the blessing of inheritance—or would he refuse to perform it? The old man was as beloved in the clan as any blood relative. How could she shun him in taking the title and keep peace in the clan afterward? He would be within his rights to leave.

"Meal," Mriy shouted, judging that the sun was high enough to be called noon. She had to admit, it was refreshing not to look at a chrono to tell the time. She slung the knapsack off her back and rummaged around to find her jerky. It was poor fare, but sat easy in the stomach. With wild game, there was always the risk that the animal was sick or had some foulness to it. Not to mention the wasted time in hunting quarry beside their prize.

"Kubu hungry!" Kubu chimed in, bounding back from one of the side excursions that had become his hedge against boredom.

"You've eaten twice since breakfast," Tanny replied. "Remember the snow hare? Remember the beaver?"

"The beaver was very wet," Kubu replied, nodding. "The bunny was yummy. Kubu still hungry."

"Well, you'll have to find your own while we walk, because I don't think we've got enough in the supplies to keep up with you."

"Who'd have thought he'd get fat running fifty kilometers a day and hunting for his own meals?" Esper asked. She dropped her knapsack, and it barely dented the snow.

"He's not getting fat," Tanny countered. "He's growing."

"What is that?" Mriy asked, ignoring the discussion of the dog and pointing to Esper's knapsack.

"My gear," Esper replied. "I couldn't make Tanny carry it two days in a row."

"Let me see that," Mriy said. She stalked over and hefted it by the straps. It was feather-light. Then she unclasped the flap and looked inside. It carried all that it ought to have; Esper hadn't ditched her supplies in a gully somewhere as Mriy had initially suspected. "How?" She shoved the knapsack into Esper's arms.

Esper dropped it in the snow once more. "Magic."

She had been speaking too often with Roddy and Carl. Their snide sarcasm was rubbing off. "We are not allowed modern devices on the hunt. Whatever anti-grav you snuck into it, turn it off."

"Ma-gic," Esper replied. "Hocus pocus. Dark arts. Mort was exaggerating when he called me a wizard, but he *has* started teaching me a few things."

Mriy picked up the knapsack once more. "You did this? Not Mort?"

"Last night it weighed a ton," Esper said. "After I got the fire to work, I figured I'd have a go at making the gear lighter. It's not so hard keeping up anymore, but I must say, you've got awfully long legs."

The human pulled out a food bar from her pocket and unwrapped it. The contents let out a whiff of factory-processed chemical flavorings that seemed out of place in the mountains.

"What is that?" Mriy asked, leaning in to sniff at it. "It smells like fruit." She was no expert at non-protein foodstuffs, but had grown accustomed to some of the smells while aboard the *Mobius*.

"It's actually six kinds of fruit, plus all the vitamins and minerals a woman's body needs," Esper recited. "It's a delicious part of a balanced diet."

Mriy's eyes narrowed. "I've heard the adverts," she muttered. It was a Snakki-Bar, one of those lazy human foods. They supposedly did all the work of three meals, but tasted awful and weren't satisfying.

Esper shrugged. "I know you don't like them. Trying one was enough. But I can't eat that stuff you brought, and I can hardly think about Kubu's meals without losing mine."

"How much of that magic did Mort teach you?" Mriy asked. A plan was forming. Maybe they were not the weak pack after all.

Esper backed away a step. "Ooooh no. I see that look. I'm not a *wizard* wizard. I'm not even a pretend wizard. I'm just learning a few things. I'm not making anyone's fur fall out or pulling knives out of people's hands. I can still lose an argument with a campfire."

"You can still cause painful hunger with a touch," Mriy said. The human was speaking in false modesty; she had killed with her magic.

"As a last resort," Esper replied. "For defense only." She took another bite of her Snakki-Bar.

"Right," Mriy said. "Defend the kill. Defend honor. Win the hunt." She clapped Esper on the shoulder. "You'll do fine when the time comes. Eat up. This won't be a long break." Esper coughed something in response, but it was lost in a mouthful of mealy, meatless food substitute.

The holovid was in azrin, which made it hard to follow. One of the occasionally annoying features of the translation charms that all the crew wore was that they didn't translate what the wearer could already understand. Since Mort's understanding of the Jiara dialect was better suited to slow conversations, he was having trouble keeping up. It wasn't that he cared what happened to the two azrin mercenaries trapped behind enemy lines on some generic extrasolar planet—well, maybe he cared a little—it was that everyone else in the room understood and he didn't.

Being the dumbest one in the room was a splinter in Mort's craw. It didn't matter that it was the dialog to a holovid with a title that translated roughly to "Two Deaths Died Well." Mort had written off the two main characters from the opening title shot. It was more that these brutish, oafish savages had one up on him in the brains department. He had always preferred a shutout victory, especially when dealing with people he had already cataloged among his mental inferiors.

"How long these hunts usually last?" Mort asked in a down moment. The two protagonists were reloading science thingamajigs into their guns.

"Hmm? What?" Frouniy asked. He was the nearest Yrris to Mort, at the back of the viewing room.

"I said—"

But there was a huge explosion in the holo-field, and the noise drowned him out as the Yrrises cheered. Mort tucked his hands into the pocket of his sweatshirt and slouched down. He didn't care what happened to the two doomed azrins on the holovid. Given the unimaginative title, they were going to die well, and that was apparently the important thing. Mort didn't need to see the ending.

With a subtle suggestion to the universe that electro-whozamawhatchits didn't need to be shooting light all over the place, the holo-projector flickered and gave out. There were mixed groans and shouts of outrage from Mort's fellow viewers. One whose name Mort hadn't asked got up and popped open the access panel to check inside as his kin badgered him with questions and suggested methods of diagnosing the problem. After a minute or two, the suggestions died down and left a sulking impatience in their wake.

Never one to let an opportunity pass, Mort struck up a conversation to fill in the silence. "So, how long is everyone expecting this hunt to last?"

This time, Frouniy was not too distracted to answer. "Tomorrow. The day after at the latest. Yariy has a good nose and can think like the prey."

"How long would it take for Mriy, if her pack was going to win?" Mort asked.

A few azrin laughs—the same hissing chuckle that Mriy used—told him that other ears were listening in. "A year," Frouniy replied. "Maybe if some poacher found our prey and didn't respect the ritual markings, they might stay out long enough that an elk might be born that looked like it. Mriy could paint it up and bring it back as a winning kill."

"Is that legal?"

"Of course it's not," Seerii said. "He jokes at you. Mriy hunts for the kill, not the track. She was four days in her ascension hunt, while her cousin Yariy did hers in an afternoon. She'll kill anything she finds, but this prey isn't a challenge for a killer. It's a tracker's race."

"What about the old fella?" Mort asked. It was odd calling Auzuma old, since he was about the age of Mort's children, but from an azrin perspective, he qualified.

"Auzuma's nose isn't young," Seerii replied. "You are old among your people. Have you not noticed the loss of scent since your youth?"

Mort chuckled. "I'm not *that* old and blast me if I'd notice the difference. If I can tell the difference between bacon, beer, and the perfume at a woman's neck, I'm all set in the scent department."

"Well, Mriy's pack is scent-blind," Seerii said. "They'll be guessing as much as anything. Mriy will be lucky to track Hrykii's pack, let alone the prey. And outnumbered five to two, even Mriy can't fight those odds."

Mort gave Seerii a shrewd squint. "You got one of those datapads that gets the omni on it? Look up a critter called *canis ultra poltidae*. I can spell it if you need; that's an old Earth dialect. I'll wait. Then you can give me a better answer about how close this contest will be."

❀ ❀ ❀

By evening, Mriy was ready to strangle Auzuma and leave him in the snow until the thaw. While Esper was managing not to fall behind, the chaplain's feet dragged slower by the hour. Hunting was a point of honor; Seerii hunted well beyond her years, but for her health and as a point of pride. A challenge was no place for the old. Desperate though she was, Mriy would have fared better with four or even three, than be weighed down with pack mates like these.

She waved to Tanny, summoning the human warrior to her side. At least Tanny would be fine for the whole of the hunt. Mriy had never seen her tire, not while she was flush with the effects of her chemicals. Though it might have been a stretch of the rules, Tanny had brought her daily doses along as part of her rations. She was the one Mriy would have to count on most until the end of the hunt.

"How is Esper?" Mriy asked as Tanny drew near, careful not to let Esper overhear.

"Tired, but holding up," Tanny replied. Mriy could hear the short breaths she took, but it was the only visible sign of Tanny's fatigue. "I'm worried about Auzuma though. I think he'd die on his feet, just to prove he won't quit."

Mriy nodded solemnly. "He might, at that." The last thing they needed was to lose more ground on Hyrkii, but she couldn't kill Auzuma either. "Break!" she shouted.

Esper slumped into the snow and looked up into the feeble sun, which gave light but little warmth. Auzuma trudged several more paces and settled in beside her. Kubu, who had disappeared more and more often as they traveled, bounded out of the forest moments later.

The five of them settled in and took a meal. Esper and Auzuma spoke of God and churches and duty. It was good to keep the two preachers facing one another, to cancel out all the noise they made. Better than them bothering her with it. Kubu had eaten something with feathers and spent the mealtime working one loose from his teeth.

"You're showing frustration," Auzuma said. They were the first words he'd spoken in her direction all day.

"We lose more ground every hour," Mriy replied.

Auzuma pointed to a mountain in their path—simple enough as mountains loomed all around. "Which one is Hyrkii's pack on now? That one? The one beyond? And which mountain hides our elk? Do you know? Does Hrykii? The hunt isn't about speed; it's about guile. Think like the elk, and be where it will be."

"Do you know where it is?" Esper asked between bites of a Snakki-Bar.

Auzuma chuckled. "I'm no elk."

"Then how do we—"

"This is pointless," Mriy snapped. "We finish eating, then get back to catching up with Hrykii. His pack will find the elk first, and we need to be there to intercept them."

Auzuma shook his head. "You sound like the fisherman who lost his spear."

Mriy huffed and swallowed back her temper. "I don't know that one," she grumbled. She knew from Auzuma's tone that she was going to hear the story or be questioned on it. Denying her ignorance would only make her look foolish.

"A young fisherman missed his thrust and hit a rock. His spear broke, and he could not find the tip. He pulled his boat onto shore and found the nearest village. But no one in the village would sell him a spear—they had no spears to sell. He asked if they could make him one, but the price they asked was more than he could afford. When he despaired of finding a replacement before the day was lost, an old man took pity on him. *I was collecting these to line a garden, but you have more need than I.* He handed the young fisherman a loose-weave bag filled with rocks. Each rock was white and smooth and big enough to fill the palm of the hand. The young fisherman thanked the old man and took the bag because he was too polite to refuse a gift. None of the rocks would make a spear tip. The bag and all the rocks inside were not worth the cost of one in trade.

"So the fisherman went back to his boat, and set off downstream toward his home. But on the way, he found a spot where fish danced at the surface, enough for three meals for his family. He anchored his boat and tried to catch them with his claws, but the fish fled when his shadow cast across the water. He tried the broken shaft of his spear, but the end was not sharp enough to skewer a fish. Then he thought of the old man's gift and tried the rocks. The bag had a woven loop for a handle, and it tied shut at the top. The fisherman tried swinging it like a club, but only splashed water over himself and into his boat. He took rocks one at a time and threw them at the fish, thinking that if he stunned one, he could pluck it from the water before it recovered. Emptying the whole bag, he hit just two fish, and both recovered before he could snatch them from the water.

"That was when he noticed that the bag was loose weave and empty, and it had a long woven handle. He dangled the bag in the water, and netted fish after fish. The old man had given him just what he needed, but the fisherman had not noticed."

"Fish come from the water?" Kubu asked. He had sat in rapt attention during the story.

"Live ones, yes," Tanny said. "The dead ones Roddy likes on his pizza come from a can."

"Are we the net?" Esper asked.

Auzuma smiled. "We are either the net, or the rocks."

"That doesn't help us," Mriy replied.

"You're using us like a spear, when we're not a spear," Auzuma said. "Knowing that must help somehow. It was exactly what a pack leader needed to hear. We are not faster than Hyrkii's hunters, nor are we stronger in a fight."

"I'm not sure of that," Mriy muttered. She was regretting bringing Auzuma along more each second. Being useless was bad enough, but to lecture her as well...

"What do we do better than him? Than his pack?" Auzuma asked.

"God's grace?" Esper guessed.

"Possibly," Auzuma allowed. "But I don't expect Him to intervene."

"Better tactics," Tanny said.

"You've hunted before, then?" Auzuma asked. "You are an expert?"

"Bet your ass I am," Tanny replied. "Not elk, either. I've been up against the Sishaji, the Plouph, and even a few Zheen. Enemies that think back at you."

"We have Kubu's nose," Esper said, straightening in her snowy seat. "We must be able to out-sniff them."

"The black beast knows how to hunt," Auzuma said. "It's in his blood. You can see it plainly."

"You're saying we should let Kubu lead?" Tanny asked.

"No," Mriy replied. She stood and looked out into the mountains, in the direction she had been expecting to find the elk. "Kubu, can you smell the elk? The one with the paint on it by the ship. The one Mort told you not to hunt yet."

Kubu nodded. "Yes. Kubu smelled it since last night. We go the right way, so Kubu thought you smelled it too."

"Well, there's that," Tanny said. "Least we're on the right track. How about we get back on it." She climbed to her feet and brushed the snow from her pants.

A slow grin caught Mriy by surprise. It was the first time since the outset where she realized a path to victory in the challenge. "No. The four of us rest. Kubu, I want you to run ahead and find the elk. Find it, and come back with it."

"Come back with it?" Tanny scoffed. "It's twice his size."

"Look at him," Mriy said, pointing to the alien canine. "He bursts with energy. There's more muscle on him than you or me. Kubu, try to bring it back, and if you can't, come back and lead us to it. Understand?"

Kubu nodded. "Yes. Kubu can't eat it, right?"

"Maybe after we give it to my mother," Mriy replied. "Now this part is important. If you run into azrin—people like Auzuma and me—run away. Don't let them catch you or hurt you. If you can prevent it, don't even let them see you. Just come right back to us; leave the elk if you have to."

"Kubu can," Kubu replied. "When can I go?" He bounced from front legs to back, tail wagging.

"Now," Mriy said.

Kubu shot off like a blaster bolt into the forest.

Kubu scooped up a mouthful of snow in full stride. Snow was the best stuff ever. It kept him cool no matter how much he ran, and it melted in his mouth so he didn't have to stop to drink. Everywhere around this place was cold, and there were yummy little animals whenever he got hungry. It was like being inside a giant refrigerator, except without the beer cans.

Kubu wished Mriy had said earlier that she didn't know where the elk was. Kubu could have told her that. The elk didn't just smell like animal; it had paint on it that smelled so different that Kubu couldn't help but notice it. There were a lot of animals around, hiding in the snow, in the trees, under the ground; but only one had the paint smell.

It was going to take a long time to get to the elk. Mriy had been going in the mostly right direction, but not the best direction. Kubu had to go around a mountain, after several failed attempts to find a way over it. There was a break for eating a bunny and another for eating a funny little animal with sharp, pointy fur that was sleeping under the snow. The sharp, pointy fur had taken a lot of chewing, and Kubu had spit some of it out for being too much work for not enough taste. But now he was moving again, and slowly closing in on the elk.

Kubu was being such a good boy. He was going to be everyone's hero when he found the elk for them. Mriy was worried that Esper and the new kitty-person were too slow, and that they'd have to go back. But now Kubu was fast, and they all could just wait for him to get the elk. Everyone was going to be very happy because of him.

There was a scent of smoke in the air. Smoke meant cooked food. Kubu had liked finding food all over the forest and the low parts of the mountains. Fresh animals were juicier, and some had surprise foods inside them. But cooking was nice, too, and the smoke tickled Kubu's nose and tugged at his attention. It wasn't as if he was going to forget about the elk; there was just a smoke smell to follow first.

As it turned out, there was more than just smoke; there were kitty-people, too. They looked like Mriy mostly. They walked on two feet, had pointy-up ears, little pink noses, and big eyes with pupils like slits. Kubu saw them before any of them looked like they noticed him. They had a pointy little house, and the smoke was coming out the top.

"Hey! We got a stray wandered in," one of the kitty-people yelled. Kubu had been wrong; at least one of them had seen him.

"Hello!" he shouted back. "It's just Kubu! You aren't the kitty-people hunting the elk Kubu is hunting. Sorry. Kubu goes now."

"Shut that damned thing up," a different kitty-person said. "Probably belongs to the humans. They keep those as pets and use them for hunting."

"Kubu isn't a pet," Kubu replied. "I stay with Mommy because she loves me, but I *am* hunting with her and Esper. I'm hunting with Mriy, too, but she isn't a human."

"Noisy creature," the first kitty-person said. He sounded mad.

Kubu realized something. They didn't have Mort, so they didn't have Mort's through-the-ear magic that let them understand Kubu. Esper had one. Mommy had one. Everyone on the ship had them—even Kubu. Kubu had gotten used to the idea that people could understand him, but these kitty-people couldn't.

One of the kitty-people had a gun. Mommy had guns, and he wasn't supposed to touch them because they were dangerous.

Now the kitty-person was aiming a gun at Kubu; it was time to do lots of running.

"Get after him," one of the kitty-people shouted. "If that thing gets back to his human masters, we're dead. Break camp and be ready to ride."

Kubu didn't know what a lot of that meant, but he gathered that they were very interested in getting him. He only hoped that they were as slow as Mriy.

❁ ❁ ❁

The *Mobius* touched down on a strip of beach, the internal gravity not even allowing a gentle thump to jostle the lone occupant. Roddy found the remote trigger for the cargo bay door and hit it, then reclined in the pilot's seat with his fingers laced behind his head. So much for his vacation. So much for peace, quiet, and solitude. The comm had come less than an hour ago; that was about as long as Roddy had been willing to let Carl stew before picking him up.

There was a rumble of pumps and hydraulics as the cargo bay ramp lowered. No one else seemed to be able to do it, but Roddy knew the ship's systems well enough that he could tell by feel or by sound when subsystems kicked on. The sound stopped, then a moment later, started again—raising the ramp.

Roddy waited.

Booted footsteps approached, slower than Carl's usual pace. "Get us out of here," Carl said in a dead-tired voice.

Roddy fired up the engines and lifted off, operating the controls with his feet. His fingers were still laced behind his head when he twisted around to face Carl. "Kicked out or quit?"

"Kicked out."

Something seemed out of place. Carl wore his usual battered leather jacket and had his stupid magic sword sheathed at his hip. But he was wearing a hat with earflaps and a pair of dark glasses. "What's with the getup? They blacken those eyes of yours, or were you training to fight in the dark."

"I'm in no mood right now to—"

"Holy shit," Roddy said, sitting up straight. "Are your eyebrows blue?"

Carl sighed and took off the glasses. His eyebrows were indeed a rather atmospheric shade of blue.

Roddy couldn't help himself; he doubled over laughing. Carl just stood there, waiting for the fit to pass. His blank, weary face made it all the more amusing. "Let me guess," Roddy said, gasping as he recovered his breath. "This is part of the sword master's teachings?"

"No," Carl said. He pulled off the hat to reveal hair that was a matching shade of blue. "I pissed him off, and he put some fucking mystic curse on me."

Roddy hardly heard the explanation, because his laughing fit redoubled. Carl looked like a cartoon character, or one of those teenyboppers who goes to pop concerts—Esper had probably dyed her hair that way when she was a kid, he guessed. And that's what Carl looked like, some teenage girl who wanted to stand out, except he still had the face of a rough-cut spacer.

"It doesn't wash out, either," Carl said when Roddy had calmed down. "I'm gonna have to ask Mort to fix it."

Roddy squinted, angling his head to catch Carl in the natural light from outside. "Is that... it is! He got the hair on your peach-fuzz face, too. It's like you're growing blue lichen."

"Oh yeah," Carl said with a sigh. "*All* my hair turned blue. The blue-fur curse, he called it. Threatened me with it when I called bullshit on some of the stuff he was teaching. Straight out of the holovids, the lot of it. If I wanted to learn dispy-do sword fighting like they do in the vids, I could download a manual from the omni. Anyway, I said I didn't have fur, so he could take his curse and suck on it. In retrospect, not a good call on my part."

"So the guy's a legit wizard?" Roddy asked.

"More wizard than swordsman, if you ask me," Carl replied. He scratched at his emerging blue stubble. "Still, once Mort gets back, I can't see him having any trouble fixing me up."

"So, what's next on the vacation tour?" Roddy asked. Hopefully, Carl would want to move on to a more relaxing pastime and leave the *Mobius* to him again.

"You kidding?" Carl asked. "No way in hell I'm going anywhere like this. Until we get Mort back to fix me up, I'm parking right here. Could use a bit of a blow off though; thinkin' maybe a little guitar might ease my troubled mind."

So much for that. "Yeah, sure," Roddy said. The ship's orbital path was already locked into the autopilot—that was about as much as he trusted the worthless computer to manage on its own. He slipped out of the pilot's chair and left the controls unattended. There would be no music to play, no peaceful view. If he was going to have any time to himself, it would be fiddling with the engines. "I tuned it. Lemme just grab it for you."

Somewhere along the way, Kubu had mostly forgotten about why he was running. It was important to get back, and he was in a big hurry, but the running was fun. Following his own scent back to Mommy was so easy that he didn't have to slow down to check which way to go. The wind in his face cooled him just as the running heated him from inside. An occasional mouthful of snow evened things out when the warming started to win out.

It was dark. The sky had lots of little lights, and the ground was all bright white, so Kubu could see. But it was time to get sleepy. The flying house didn't have good day and night like outside did. It was nice to have day and night, and night was for sleeping. Once Kubu was done running, he was going to have a nice, big sleep. Hopefully Mommy wouldn't mind sharing her food. Kubu was hungry.

Kubu couldn't remember the last time he had run so much. It was a long way back to Mommy, he realized. It had taken him a lot of time to find the little house with the kitty-people—oh, that was why Kubu was running!—but he hadn't realized how far it was all in one run.

Two growling buzzes approached from somewhere behind Kubu. He had never heard anything quite like them before. They sounded like big bugs, the kind that fly and sting, but much louder. Kubu hadn't seen any bugs. Mommy had said that bugs don't like the cold, which was another reason that the big outdoor refrigerator was the best place ever. Kubu had never liked bugs, especially the ones that flew and stung. They were hard to catch, stung the inside of his mouth, didn't taste good, and didn't fill the tummy much. There was just nothing good about bugs. With two bugs—probably very big ones—coming from behind, Kubu ran even faster.

❁ ❁ ❁

Dawn was breaking when Kubu arrived back in camp. Mriy had been just about to wake Esper and Auzuma for breakfast when the huffing and panting of the noisy beast approached. To her chagrin, he was not dragging a painted elk in his jaws.

It had probably been optimistic to think Kubu could haul a creature three times his size for kilometers over snow-covered terrain.

"Mommy-mommy-mommy," Kubu shouted as he came within sight. Tanny was already awake and raised an arm in greeting. At least *she* had the good sense not to give her location away by shouting.

"Did you find it?" Tanny asked.

Kubu pulled up a few meters from camp and cocked his head to the side. "Find it?"

"The elk," Mriy clarified. "The painted elk you were looking for."

"Kubu found kitty-people," Kubu replied. His tongue lolled from his mouth, and he hung his head.

Mriy flattened back her ears. "Az-rin. Not kitty-people." She had told Kubu a dozen times at the least. "Where are they?" This could be decisive news. If Kubu could lead them to Hrykii's hunting party, they could set up a distraction and ambush to separate them from the elk when Hrykii found it—if he hadn't already.

"They had a pointy little house with smoke," Kubu said.

Mriy felt a chill that her fur and vest could do nothing to ward off. "They had a house?"

"Who'd be living out here?" Tanny asked.

Mriy shook her head. "No one should be. This is a public hunting ground, an area a hundred times the size of Rikk Pa that should be only for hunters. Come, hunt, leave: those are the rules."

"Kubu, did they see you?" Tanny asked, bending down to one knee to look Kubu in the eye.

Kubu nodded. "Oh yes! Kubu tried to talk to them, but they didn't have through-the-ear magic, so they couldn't understand Kubu. Then they got mad and pointed guns at Kubu, so Kubu ran away."

"Well, that was smart—the running part, I mean," Tanny said. "You know you're not supposed to be talking to strangers."

"Did they follow you?" Mriy asked.

Kubu shook his head. "Just bugs. Kubu had bugs chase him, but he got away."

A sound that had no place in nature prickled Mriy's ear. It was distant, but grew louder by the second. It was a buzz, and as it drew closer she identified it. "Those weren't bugs," she snapped. "Those are snow-rollers. You led them back to us!"

"What are we up against?" Tanny asked, drawing a hunting knife. It was a soldier's reaction, and a good one, but likely inadequate.

"Poachers, trappers, squatters, fugitives," Mriy listed them off as possibilities came to mind. "If they were traditionalists, they wouldn't have vehicles. If they're not, then they'll be armed with more than knives."

"Options?"

Mriy shook her head. "Even if we had Kubu start a false trail, he still left tracks straight to us. Wake Esper and Auzuma; get them to cover."

This wasn't good. Hrykii pack was already more than a match for them. It was going to be a battle of guile against a superior force. This was more than anyone in the challenge had bartered for. Mriy headed back along Kubu's trail, taking a position on a ridge a quarter kilometer outside camp on a low rise. There just wasn't enough tree cover. Snow-rollers would slice through camp at full speed, and gun-armed occupants would have every advantage. Except possibly surprise.

Mriy worked quickly. She took rope from her knapsack and tied one end around the stump of a fallen pine. The whine of the engines continued to draw nearer. The mountain echoes played tricks with the ear that prevented her from pinning down their exact distance, but time was at a premium. Crossing Kubu's tracks in the snow, she found a standing pine and looped the rope around that as well, tying it off with a bit of slack. There was just enough play in the line for Mriy to wiggle the rope below the snow's surface and be able to pull it back up to just about the height of a snow-roller's tracks.

The snow was knee-deep and powdery. Mriy grabbed a branch as long as her body, then hunkered down in the snow. White fur was uncommon in azrins. When she was young, children had teased her about it—before she grew larger than her tormentors—but now she was thankful for a bit of natural camouflage. The buzzing continued to grow, until she could clearly make out two distinct snow-rollers. She had been off-world too long; the engines were newer models that she didn't recognize by ear. They sounded heavy duty, possibly six- or eight-seaters—if she was lucky, perhaps just four.

With the size of the approaching snow-rollers, Mriy began to worry about the rope. It was a glass-fiber composite weave, but far from indestructible. It wasn't often that she wished Roddy were around, but the laaku mechanic had a quick mind for such problems. Assume a speed for a snow-roller, its weight, its durability. The rope had a tensile strength, which Roddy would know or could estimate. Which would prevail? Would the rope halt the snow-roller, or at least slow it violently enough to eject the occupants? Would the trees even hold up to the strain?

Mriy's slapdash plan was to disable one vehicle, scavenge a weapon from the dead or injured crew, and take on the surprised survivors in the second snow-roller. Best case, the second vehicle would crash into the first, but that was asking much from a benevolent god. More likely, Mriy would die a good death, taking enough of Kubu's pursuers with her that Tanny could find a way to deal with the rest.

The engines grew thunderous as the snow-rollers sped toward her position. They must have been following Kubu's tracks, with no effort to head him off or circle around. Good. She had counted on that. Just as she prepared to use her branch to lift the rope into place, one of the engines cut to idle, then the other.

"Come on out," a voice called, echoing in the mountain air. "Got you on thermals. You'd have to be down there long enough to freeze to hide from me."

Mriy let go of her branch and drew her fighting knives. She had bought them off-world, and had never gotten a chance to use them on prey. It looked like today was not going to be the first, either. "Who are you?" she shouted back over her shoulder, her back against the base of her rope's anchor tree.

"We are the sons and daughters of Meyang," came the reply. "I am Hraim."

"Shit!" Mriy muttered in English. It was such a rich language for cursing. But now wasn't the time to panic. These were rebels, the self-proclaimed saviors of azrin-kind. They were dedicated to evicting the human occupation with a mixture of stubborn disobedience, propaganda, and a charmingly naive misunderstanding of planetary logistics.

It wasn't time to fight. She was outnumbered, and her ambush had failed thanks to a pair of thermal-imaging lenses. It was time to Carl them. Unfortunately, this meant Mriy would have to play the role of Carl. *Lie, and if the lie doesn't work, lie some more.* It was worth a shot. "I'm on a ritual hunt," Mriy answered back, still not emerging from behind her tree. It was one of Carl's tenets not to lie about the obvious and easily verified. *Motives. Lie about motives.* "My chaplain and I found a pair of humans and took them prisoner."

"Where are they?" Hraim demanded.

"Don't shoot," Mriy said. "I'm standing up. I am armed only for the hunt." She stepped from behind the tree and showed the rebels as she sheathed both knives. There were eight of them traveling in a pair of six-seater snow-rollers. Each was armed with a blaster rifle, some off-world brand she didn't recognize—probably from a non-ARGO world, if they weren't hypocrites. All, of course, were azrin.

Mriy turned her back on the rebels, facing camp. "Auzuma, you can come out. They're our people. Bring the human prisoners." Hopefully at least one of the three of them had the sense to play along. Tanny probably. She had known Carl and his ways for a long time.

A minute later, Auzuma emerged from the distant trees, herding Tanny and Esper in front of him. Neither of the humans were wearing the sheathes for their hunting knives. Good. Hopefully they had hidden the weapons under the snow and concealed them well.

Hraim's rebels aimed weapons at the pair of humans. That was when things went over the ledge. "What were they doing when you—"

His question was cut off by a snarl that had Mriy reaching for her weapons by reflex. She dropped into a ready crouch before she saw Kubu charge from the forest, teeth bared. "No, guns at Mommy!" What it must have sounded like to the rebels, Mriy couldn't imagine.

"Turn to stone, dog!" Hraim shouted, his rifle aimed in Kubu's direction.

Whether it was a poor understanding of idiom, a protectiveness of Tanny, or simple canine bloodlust, Kubu didn't falter. Neither did Hraim. The rebel fired a single shot, and a splat of plasma caught Kubu in the shoulder. But Kubu only stumbled into the snow for a second. He came up howling, hobbling, and heading straight for Hraim. Mriy had never seen a human get up after being shot with a plasma bolt, even a non-lethal blast to a limb. She doubted she could muster the strength to stand after taking a shot like that, and she'd never have been able to run.

A second shot caught Kubu in the chest. He let out a lone, shrieking whimper and collapsed, skidding to a limp halt in the snow.

Carl settled into the copilot's seat. His guitar sounded all wrong thanks to Roddy fiddling with it—too perfect, no soul—but it was technically the laaku's, so he couldn't complain. Without a few riffs to relax him, Carl decided to see about scrounging up some work for the *Mobius*. Meyang might have been a backwater with an ARGO garrison parked in orbit, but sometimes those were just the right ingredients for someone to need the sort of service the *Mobius* offered.

But the first thing that struck Carl as he looked out the cockpit window was the ship's attitude. They were nose first to the planet, pointing like a hunting dog with a gift for stating the obvious. Meyang filled the view, like a naked Earth without its cities. Carl leaned over to the pilot's controls and feathered the maneuvering thrusters, flipping the *Mobius* around without altering their orbit. He took a long, deep breath as the welcoming stars greeted him. "We'll be back out there soon enough. You fellas aren't going anywhere, right?" Carl had been born on a starship and lived most of his life on them. A planet was just an asteroid with pretension.

"Now, let's see," he mumbled to himself, browsing the ship's computer from the copilot's terminal. "Meyang, Meyang, Meyang—what do you people need to get off-world?" The omni was filled with every bit of useless information anyone felt compelled to share over public computing. From ancient historical translations, to ARGO treaty terms, to complaints about the local music scene—if someone saw fit to log it to an unsecured network, it was on the omni. Slogging through the mush of data wasn't Carl's specialty, but anyone with a decent education could muddle through it.

It was boring. Carl was bored. The omni went on and on forever—that was sort of its thing. Over the two hours he searched, he learned fact after useless fact about Meyang and azrin culture. It went in through his eyes and leaked out his ears. For the most part, azrins were retroverts, xenophobes, and paupers. Anything new, expensive, or off-world was a tough sell. They resented ARGO—though who could blame them. The ones who worked closely with the "occupiers" were widely derided. A tech-free lifestyle was considered the ideal—which Carl found an ironic sentiment to be posting on the omni.

With nothing better to go on, Carl reverted to the old-fashioned method. He took out an ad. There was an art to advertising illegal services. As with many cons, it relied on the way a potential customer would read it, as opposed to an honest citizen. Turn your back on a stack of hardcoin terras, and a corrupt bureaucrat knows to take the bribe. Tell a potential client that you can "get anything he needs," and he'll know you're willing to ship contraband. But the same way an honest filing clerk will leave your terras alone, an honest client will just think you're being enthusiastic and accommodating.

But with savvy ARGO agents out there watching, it took more care to craft an advert. They *weren't* the honest sorts, which is how they did their job. Overplay it just a little and a captain could end up with a ringer on board—like one Mr. Bryce Brisson, or whatever-the-hell his real name was.

Light freighter leaving orbit soon. Space left in hold. Prefer small, high-value cargo.

That sounded about right. It sounded like a captain wanting to squeeze some terras into the last few cubic meters of his hold before heading off-world. Really, aside from tremble-handed cowards, who *didn't* want to carry small, high-value cargo? But to someone desperate to get a quarantined plant or a thousand-year-old cultural artifact out of the system, the implication was clear: *pay me enough and I'll sneak something past customs for you.*

Carl smiled to himself, satisfied with a job well done. Let the suckers planetside do the work themselves. He had a guitar to tune until it had some soul back in it.

"Kubu, no!" Esper shouted. He fell into the snow and didn't move. All thoughts of their ruse of being prisoners fled her mind. She rushed through the shin-deep snow, stumbling to her hands and knees twice on her way to reach Kubu's side.

He was breathing quick and shallow. A gaping hole in his chest, charred around the edges, leaked red blood onto the snow. Another in his shoulder did likewise. Esper wanted to be sick, but there was no time for that. She shut her eyes and placed her hands on Kubu's side. "It's OK. It's going to be OK," she whispered.

He whined softly. "Kubu hurts."

She had learned her healing spell in a rhyme as a girl. It seemed silly at the time, but she knew from Mort that asking was a part of receiving. *"Cuts close, bruises fade; three weeks healing done today; bones knit, pains ease; cleanse the body of disease."* She repeated it in Latin, remembering Mort's advice that the universe responded better the older the languages. *"Comprimare vulnus, livores defluet; tres septimanas sanando fit hodie; os implexae, lenire dolores; purgare corpus morbus."* In church Latin, it felt like an invocation to God.

Kubu writhed beneath her hands. His whining grew stronger, pained. "Hungry! Kubu hungry." She looked down and saw a pair of blood-crusted scars with missing fur, stark pink against Kubu's black fur.

Esper plunged her arms into the snow and wrapped them around Kubu's neck, engulfing him in a hug. "Oh, Kubu. You're going to be all right."

He squirmed in her grasp, his high-pitched keening causing a pain in Esper's ears. "Hungry."

"Of course," Esper mumbled. Fumbling in her pocket, she pulled out two Snakki Bars she'd been keeping handy for mid-hike snacks. Kubu took a quick sniff and gobbled them from her hands before she could even take her gloves off to unwrap them.

"What did she do?" Hraim demanded.

"She is holy," Mriy replied. "A priestess among the humans. God listens to her prayers."

That might have been a bit of a stretch. By Esper's quick count that was a lie, a used-to-be, and an I-don't-know. Had it been God she'd just spoken to, or some less deific entity that held sway over physics and impossibility.

"We are on a ritual hunt," Auzuma said, drawing the attention of the rebels, but not the aim of their rifles. "We did not come to hunt humans, but humans are what we found. I am a chaplain, so I couldn't abide the killing of a priestess."

Hraim nodded. "I won't keep you from your hunt. We have contacts. We can get a ransom for them. But not for the dog. Those things are good for nothing but hunting our people. One fewer bloodhound, one less worry for us." He strode through the snow like a king—or a warlord—his head high, weapon held ready to pronounce sentence.

Esper threw herself over Kubu, who still lay in the snow after devouring his snack. "You won't hurt him!"

Hraim stood right over her, prodding with the muzzle of his blaster rifle. "Move aside. Obey and you'll see your people again. Defy me, and holy woman or not, I'll shoot him right through you."

Esper hadn't been a criminal long enough to be used to people pointing weapons at her. The image of Kubu's charred wound flashed across her mind. She wasn't built like him, wasn't half muscle, half sinew and bone. A blaster wound would be fatal before she could even begin to heal herself.

"*Ignus*," she muttered. Tempting as it was to take out her wrath on the azrin rebel, she turned her thoughts to melting the snow around her. "*Ignus*," she repeated. A thin fog rose around her.

"What are you doing?" Hraim asked. "Stop it. Stop it at once."

"Shoot me," Esper said, neither raising her head nor looking at the azrin. She continued to shield Kubu with her body.

"Dumb human, I don't want to—"

"God will protect me!" Esper shouted. She wondered how many of the rebels understood English, the language of their enemies.

Hraim hissed a long sigh, heavy with disgust. "Fine."

Click. Esper cringed, but nothing happened. *Click. Click.* Esper's use of magic so close to the rifle had fouled the scientific principles it replied upon.

"What's going on?" Hraim demanded. "Zaulau, toss me your gun." Another of the azrin rebels complied, and the weapon slapped into Hraim's waiting hands.

Esper buried her face against Kubu's flank. "*Ignus.*"

Click... click click click. "Blasted things. What's—"

"Going on?" Auzuma asked. "Just as she said, Hraim: God protects her. See why we did nothing to them?"

Esper let out a sigh and was glad not to have been standing. She likely would have toppled to the snow with her legs turned to rubber beneath her.

Hraim gestured with his rifle in Tanny's direction. "What about the other one?"

"Who's to take a chance like that?" Auzuma replied. "Not me. Not Mriy. This is a ritual hunt, not a rebellion. We stand together, but in two different places. This is your battlefield, but our hunting ground."

"We'll take them off your hands, so you can continue your hunt," Hraim said.

"Do you have a fire we could share?" Mriy asked. Something in the way she said it sounded stiff and formal. What Esper didn't know about ritual hunts could have filled a book—and somewhere on the omni, it probably did. New aspects popped up every time the wind shifted. Did a fire hold special significance, or was Mriy simply begging for hospitality?

Hraim glanced over at the snow-rollers. "We have a permanent camp set up. You can sleep in beds and have a fire for the night. Make your human prisoners understand that their lives depend on their behavior. And if that mongrel so much as looks at me, I'm shooting it and leaving it for the crows."

Mriy repeated the instructions in English, knowing full well all of them had understood Hraim just fine. Of course, the less he knew about them the better.

As azrin hands hauled her into the lead snow-roller, Esper wondered just how much Carl might be willing—or able—to pay for her release.

❀ ❀ ❀

The call wasn't long in coming. "Yo, *Mobius* here," Carl said into the comm. He set down his guitar between the pilot and copilot's seats. He couldn't remember how to play the outro to "Layla" anyway, so nothing of value was lost.

"*Is comm secure?*" a voice with a thick azrin accent asked.

"Sure," Carl replied, kicking his feet up onto the control console. "How about your end?"

"*As well, mine is,*" the azrin replied. "*I see face. You transmit.*"

There was an old belief among humankind that you could tell a man was lying by looking into his eyes. You wouldn't do business over a comm or with a guy wearing dark glasses. That was for suckers. Modern psychology said that was all bunk, and Carl knew just *how* bunk better than most. Apparently that tidbit of modern thinking hadn't reached Meyang just yet.

"I really prefer voice only," Carl replied. If no one saw your face, you could claim in court that it could have been anyone forging your voice imprint.

"*My job, eleventy thousand terra,*" the azrin replied. Carl supposed that was a lot like 11,000. "*You. Face. Or no terra.*"

Carl rolled his eyes and reached for the button to switch on the vid feed. "You're the boss. Happy now?"

"Your fur. Blue?" the azrin asked.

"Yeah, it's a funny story. I was—"

"No cursed fur," the azrin replied. *"Deal off."* The comm went dead.

"Yeah, well you're no prize yourself," Carl snapped, addressing a comm panel that was no longer transmitting. "Fuck. He probably wanted us to transport sentient eggs, or cloned scientists, or some other bullshit. When the hell is that azrin cultural enrichment field trip going to end? I'm sick of this flea-trap planet and its superstitious felid residents."

He looked around the cockpit. "Where the hell did I leave that hat?"

❀ ❀ ❀

The rebels' refuge was nicer than Kubu had let on. Given Kubu's communication skills, that might have been expected, but this went beyond understatement. The rebels had built along a hillside, using the soil for insulation. Despite needing a chimney for their fire, they were reasonably hidden from thermal scans.

Mriy and Auzuma were led inside, while Tanny, Esper, and Kubu were herded into one of the pens where the rebels kept wild game caught alive. The lone mountain goat that had occupied it before their arrival was slaughtered and brought inside for the night's meal.

Hraim's rebels gave Mriy a wide berth, but a few spoke briefly and quietly with the chaplain. It seemed that he was the less intimidating of the two, or perhaps Hraim had wanted to handle her himself. He came to sit with her, bringing two goat legs. He offered one to Mriy and took a bite from the other. "So, what sort of hunt was this?"

Mriy saw no reason to lie, this time. "My nephew was appointed heir while I was away. Three years off-world is not abandonment of my duties. I challenged to make the claim my own."

Hraim pointed to Auzuma with his dinner. "And him? Seems old for a hunt."

"My nephew brought the clan's guardian. I wanted an even match. If we fight for the prize elk, let him match against the chaplain, while I face the guardian."

"Bold," Hraim replied, nodding. "Very old thinking. Sounds like something I'd expect one of mine to do."

"What about them?" Mriy asked. "What are the sons and daughters of Meyang doing so far from cities? These lands are meant for hunts."

"And we hunt them," Hraim replied. "That goat you're gnawing is no pen-raised cattle. You can feel the strength in those muscles as your teeth tear through. We're too few to fight back against the humans, but we won't let them turn us into their kind. Weak. Store fed. Reliant on technology. Not us."

Mriy noticed that many of the rebels were young, not much older than Hrykii. They hung on Hraim's words, though none moved close enough to join the conversation. They hung on the fringes of the common dining hall, watching.

"How much do you make selling hostages to the occupiers?" Mriy asked. It was a question she'd never have considered three years before, but the *Mobius* and her wandering times had taught her to think of the costs of things. The worlds made much more sense when you saw how money flowed. Desperate thieves and dishonest businessmen had seemed such strange creatures before she had met so many of them in person.

"Most of them get 10,000 terras per head," Hraim replied. "Hard to spend, though, since they look for us in the cities. This holy woman, maybe we'll get 20,000 for her. Some church must miss her by now."

"The One Church," Mriy added.

"All the better," Hraim replied. "Those fiends spit on God's commandments and have more wealth than the Profit Minya, blessed is his name. Be good to have some of that back from them. They owe more than they can ever repay."

"What of food, shelter for the night?" Mriy asked.

Hraim yawned. He had finished most of his goat leg as they spoke, and the weight of sleep was heavy on his eyes. "We've penned humans overnight before. They're dressed for it. We've never had one freeze, yet. And they won't starve in a single night. I don't want the dining hall smelling like burned meat."

Mriy finished her meal, and a young rebel with lusty eyes led her to her borrowed sleeping quarters. The offer of his own was plain in his manner—the low growls, the touch of his hand on her back—but Mriy ignored him. She had bigger problems, because no one was going to be paying for Tanny or Esper's rescue.

❀ ❀ ❀

Carl woke to the sound of the comm built into his datapad. He hummed along with the opening bars of "Smoke on the Water" as he fumbled to accept the call.

"Whazzit?" he mumbled, rubbing his eyes.

"*This the* Mobius?" a voice on the other end asked. It was human, which was a damn sight better than fur-fearing locals.

"Yup," Carl replied. There was a long pause. "This is the part where you tell me why you called."

"I... I've got an object—let's call it an item—and this item needs delivering," the voice on the comm said.

"Listen, pal," Carl said, stopping to yawn and stretch. "I can tell you're new at this, so let me help you out. You tell me what you've got—a box, a sack, a herd of somethingorothers, a person—how big it is, how much it weighs, whether I need to feed it or keep it cold or whatever. Then you tell me where to bring it and how soon you need it there. You offer me a price and we haggle until we agree on a number. This isn't a holovid; it's just business."

"*Oh.*"

"Take a minute," Carl said. "Collect yourself. I just woke up, and I gotta piss." Carl muted the comm.

When he came back, his contact was better prepared. "*It's a box. Weighs 0.65 kilos. Fits in hand. I need it delivered to a ship waiting at an astral depth of 3.80, just outside the Meyang System.*"

"Sounds easy enough," Carl replied. It was a local drop-off. The poor slob on the other end of the comm probably worried that he'd get searched at customs, and his buyer probably had warrants out on his ship and crew.

"*I need it there by 7:00 tonight,*" the voice said.

Carl blew out a long breath and scanned the datapad for the time. It was 9:32 AM, but the *Mobius* kept to Earth Standard Time. "That local? What's it in Earth Standard?"

There was another long pause. "*I'm two hours ahead of Earth Standard, so 5:00 PM for you. Can you manage by then?*"

"Sure," Carl replied. It was seven and a half hours for a quick pickup and drop-off. "What's the job pay?"

"*How does 50,000 sound?*"

It was times like this that Carl was glad he didn't leave the comm open while he listened. Otherwise his client would have heard him choke on the beer he had just cracked open.

He finished coughing and sputtering and composed himself. Fifty thousand was just another day scanning in on a time clock, he told himself. "Yeah, I guess it's easy enough. I don't have anything else going on today. Transmit coordinates, and I'll come make the pickup."

Carl brushed his teeth as the client worked on that, then called down to the engine room and woke Roddy up, letting him know about the job. A pickup the two of them could manage just fine. For the delivery, they were going to need Mort. The edge of the system at a weird astral depth was child's play with Mort along. Without him, they might as well have been sitting atop the ship's hull with oars for all the good it would do them.

Settling into the pilot's seat, Carl put them on a heading for a place the azrins called Ishiy Pa, but which ancient Earthlings had named Athens—give or take a hundred kilometers. They'd be there in minutes, but that end of the trip wasn't the trouble. He found a comm ID for the *Yinnak* and put in a call.

"*Who calls?*" an azrin voice demanded.

"I need to speak with Mort, the human wizard you've got staying with you," Carl said.

"*Who. Calls?*" the azrin said more slowly.

"Shit. Doesn't speak English," Carl muttered. Not for the first time, he wished more people wore translator-charmed earrings. Understanding people who didn't think you knew their language came in handy once in a while, but nowhere near as often as it was a royal pain in the ass. He dusted off the few words of azrin he'd picked up and keyed the comm. "No. Azrin. Speak. Human."

"*You wait,*" the azrin replied. Carl breathed a sigh of relief.

"*Who is this?*" a new voice asked.

"This is Carl Ramsey, captain of the *Mobius*. I need to speak with Mort, the wizard that—"

"Mort!" the azrin shouted. Carl flinched and pulled the datapad away from his ear, though by the echo, it had not been shouted directly into the comm. "*Some ship captain wants to speak with you.*"

"*Bleeding blue blazes, Carl,*" Mort's familiar voice carried annoyance clearly over the comm. "*We were watching a holovid of the Mongol invasion of China. I finally convinced them that their local fictional productions were shit. I still think they're mostly watching to see gruesome human deaths, but it's an improvement over the wooden acting and fairy-tale plots their holos are crammed with.*"

"Glad you're having fun, but I've got us a job," Carl said. "It's hot to go, and I need a wizard for it. Delivery is in astral space, just outside the system. There's always a chance we might wear out our welcome in the process, so I'd like to get everyone rounded up before we head off. We've got just over seven hours left to make the drop, and I'll be picking it up in the next fifteen minutes. I can get to you in under an hour."

"*Don't rush on my account. Our intrepid hunters aren't back yet.*"

"They've got to be just about done by now. Any chance you can prod things along?"

"*I came down to prevent that sort of thing, not cause it.*"

"Yeah, but this is just a family matter," Carl replied. "I've got business up here."

"*Head on over,*" Mort replied. "*But I'm not leaving until they get back—on their own.*"

Carl punched the comm hard enough that he worried he might have broken it. "Dammit! Why do you have to act like such a fucking..." Carl searched for the word, but nothing described a wizard who gummed up the works. If Mriy wanted to inherit a chunk of this blasted planet when her mother died, fine. But it was getting in the way of easy money—which was never as easy as advertised.

Esper had never been in a cage before. It was nowhere to be found on her list of things she wished to experience in her lifetime. She might have listed setting foot on an Earth-like world or two, but not setting face on them. If there was one good thing to be said about the animal pen where she and Tanny had been locked up, it was that it had been kept clear of snow. That and the wall of snow that came right up to the bars on one side shielded them from the worst of the wind.

"Hold still," Tanny scolded. They were lying back to back, where Tanny could reach the cord that tied Esper's wrists together while her own were similarly bound. "I've almost got a grip on it... almost... shit!"

Tanny was breathing hard, her huffing as loud as Kubu's panting from the next cage over. He seemed none the worse for wear after his ordeal, other than being hungry—not that he wasn't always hungry. A part of Esper had doubted he would survive those horrible wounds. She wasn't a miracle worker; her magic only sped natural healing. That meant that if someone had kept Kubu from bleeding to death or suffering infection, he'd eventually have pulled through on his own. She could hardly imagine running into a full-grown version of him, wild and hungry, and fully able to devour her in a bite or two.

"Give me a minute, and I'll try again," Tanny said. She twisted and rolled to face Esper's back. "I need another look at those knots."

"Maybe it's special cord," Esper said. "It might be meant to cut and not untie."

"I don't care what it's meant for. I just want to get loose."

"What do we do if we get ourselves untied?"

Tanny heaved a sigh. "We'll figure that out if we get that far."

"I could try magic," Esper suggested.

"Mort showed you a trick for getting loose from something like this?"

"Not exactly," Esper replied. "But he showed me the general principles of arguing with the universe. I could improvise."

"Let's save that as a last resort, all right?"

Tanny flipped back-to-back again with Esper, and the tugging at her wrists resumed. Esper gritted her teeth as the cord dug into her flesh and rubbed the raw wound. She didn't say anything about it to Tanny; Tanny was doing everything she could to help them escape. She didn't need Esper whining and complaining the whole while.

"Mort did teach me how to set things on fire," Esper said softly as Tanny worked. "But I don't think I could to it to a person. I... I just thought you might need to know that."

"Figured as much," Tanny said between grunts of exertion. Esper could barely feel her hands, with the cord cutting off circulation. She could only imagine Tanny's struggles to untie a knot with hers still bound. "Just wish they'd used a fiber rope instead of this synthetic shit. I'd stomach some burns to get loose, but not the temperatures it would take to melt this stuff."

Esper kept quiet and tried to focus her thoughts anywhere but on the pain in her wrists and ankles, but the latter wasn't so bad through the fabric of her pants. She couldn't tell whether the numb feeling down in her feet was lack of circulation or the cold. The azrins had taken their boots.

The tugging at Esper's wrists finally stopped. Tanny fell back, panting. "Not gonna happen. Even if I could get a grip, my fingers are too numb to loosen the knot."

"Magic's turn?" Esper asked. "What should I try?"

"Nothing that can explode or burn," Tanny replied. "I dunno, maybe make the cord stretchy or brittle. Mort doesn't usually go in for half-measures, so I'm guessing here."

"I'll try stretchy," Esper replied. She closed her eyes and envisioned the cord being rubber—soft, pliable, elastic. She described the imagined cord in detail, the words kept inside her head. The universe would hear her either way. When there was no immediate effect, she began again. Then a third time and a fourth. By the fifth she was growing cross with the universe, and told it so. By the sixth recitation, the universe had just about had it with her nagging.

A jolt shook the ground and rattled their cage, though not enough to damage it or break loose the lock. Esper flinched; she would have jumped if she hadn't been tied hand and foot.

"What was that?" Tanny asked. It was the first time Esper had heard a tremble in her voice.

"I argued with the universe, and I think it just said 'no.'"

Mriy crept through the darkened hideout. The rebels kept no sentry, no night watch. And why should they? Their prisoners were caged and secured. Their two guests were on a ritual hunt. At worst, they might have suspected Mriy and Auzuma to depart before dawn to resume their hunt. Waking their hosts would have been far more rude than departing without a farewell.

Mriy's makeshift room had been a corner of a supply closet. Auzuma had been given space in the dining room, with a bed of blankets not far from the hearth fire. It was a concession to his old age and a sign of respect from the rebels. A young warrior enjoyed cold air for sleeping, but old bones liked to feel a fire's warmth.

Auzuma snored, curled up head-to-feet, with one arm over his face. Mriy approached with a hunter's stealth, as if he were prey. Her first instinct was to clamp a hand over his mouth to silence him while she assured him who she was. It was a human's holovid plan. It might have worked on human sleepers, but if she did that to Auzuma, old warrior instincts might have taken over and she could have found herself brawling in the middle of the room before Auzuma realized what he was doing. Instead, she whispered.

"Auzuma."

An ear twitched, but he showed no other reaction.

"Auzuma," Mriy repeated, leaning closer but not daring any louder voice. He stirred, and she spoke his name once more.

An eye opened, the wide pupil narrowing to a slit in the firelight. "What is it?" he asked in a whisper that matched her own.

"The hunt is over. I have failed. We're going to release the humans and get out of here."

Auzuma twisted his head until both his eyes could look into hers. He held her gaze for just a moment, then gave a solemn nod. Mriy swallowed back a lump in her throat, knowing that she hadn't admitted until then—even to herself—that she would not prevail over Hrykii.

Auzuma followed her without another word. When the old chaplain reached for his knapsack, Mriy put a restraining hand on his shoulder. She shook her head when he turned a questioning look in her direction. The gear was not worth the risk of the noise it might make in the taking.

The night air was calm, but cold enough to cut through fur. By the moonlight, the live-prey cages were easy to spot, some fifty meters from the nearest building, where the smells and sounds of the animals would be less distracting. Out in the open air, there was less need for quiet.

"You find the snow-rollers," Mriy said. "However many they have, we take them all or disable any we have to leave behind. I'll release Tanny and Esper."

"Kubu too!" Kubu shouted, his deep voice echoing in the mountain air. Mriy had forgotten how keen Kubu's ears were. He had overheard her hushed voice from forty meters away.

"Yes, you too," she hissed. "Be silent."

She hurried through the snow as Auzuma disappeared around the side of the rebels' main domicile in search of snow-rollers. There were a dozen cages, each a mesh of composite steel bars with gaps barely large enough to fit a finger through. The animals occupying the rest of the cages stirred as Mriy approached the cage with Tanny and Esper bound on the cold ground within.

"Mriy, praise the Lord," Esper whispered. "Get us out of here."

"What did you think I was out here for?" Mriy muttered as she examined the lock. It was a simple padlock with a DNA reader. Such trivial security seemed negligent, but the cages were mainly used for livestock. Mriy pressed a finger to the pad of the reader, and the locked opened.

Dragging Tanny and Esper out into the open to get better access to their bindings, Mriy drew a hunting knife and sawed through the cords. Esper gasped in relief when the pressure came off her wrists, twisting and stretching and flinching when she rubbed at the raw, bleeding wounds that were left. She stood clumsily, shaking feeling back into numb feet. Tanny was more stoic and less patient. She grabbed a spare knife from Mriy as soon as her hands were free and quickly snapped the cord tying her own ankles together.

"This one won't open," Esper whispered loudly. She was crouched at Kubu's cage, pressing her own finger to the lock as Mriy had done earlier.

"Azrin DNA," Mriy said. She crossed over and pressed her finger to the reader. The lock popped. "Anyone here can unlock it except you two—three." She added the last after Kubu opened his mouth to object.

The canine had not been bound. Given his quadrupedal anatomy and the fact that his dewclaws barely functioned as thumbs, there was little need to bind him. He sprang from his cage with his tail wagging, but remained obediently silent.

A knife blade caught the moonlight, flashing a signal that caught Mriy's eye. Auzuma waved to her, summoning the group to his location around the side of the compound. But Mriy's keen eyes caught something else as well, approaching from the woods. An azrin form was watching them from behind a tree. It seemed that Hraim might have been cautious enough to post a guard, after all.

"Run for it," Mriy whispered. "I'll catch up." She pointed toward Auzuma and hurried Esper along with a shove in that direction.

"We won't leave without you," Esper insisted, catching her balance and stopping dead in her tracks in the snow.

"You're not fit to stay and help," Mriy replied. "You have no boots. You'll freeze if you don't get to the snow-rollers and get out of here."

"Just hurry," Tanny said, grabbing Esper by the arm.

"Don't worry. Leave without me if you must. They won't kill one of their own kind," Mriy said. She dropped into a crouch and headed for the tree line.

It was then that the sentry must have realized he had been spotted. "Turn to stone, traitor!" he shouted. When he came up from his crouch, the sentry was aiming a blaster rifle at her.

Mriy did as ordered, stopping in her tracks. He was too far to rush, too close to miss his shot. Only seconds earlier she had claimed that these rebels—these sons and daughters of Meyang—would not kill her. She still believed that to be true. But what she couldn't admit in front of Esper was that, short of killing, there was no limit to the harm they might do a traitor. Mriy's best ally was the sentry's own reluctance to fire what was undeniably a deadly weapon at her.

"I tried to stop them," Mriy said, carefully keeping her hands out wide and in plain sight. "The holy one used some spell on me. She's only just now far enough that I could break free of it."

The sentry stepped out from behind the cover of his tree and into better light. She struggled to recall his name—Rrumlau, the quiet one with the shoulders like an ox. He kept his rifle aimed at Mriy's midsection, but remained silent.

The growl of a snow-roller's engine echoed in the night. It was joined by another a second later. Those engines revved and hummed, then quieted.

Mriy turned her head in the direction of the noise. "They're getting away!" she shouted. "They won't come past us. They'll go the long way around. Hurry if you want to get a shot off before they're gone."

Rrumlau looked from Mriy to the distant sound of the snow-rollers and back again. He snarled. "Try nothing foolish." With that, he rushed off in the direction of the fading engine noise.

Mriy drew a hunting knife, took aim, and threw. The blade flipped end over end, catching Rrumlau a glancing blow on the back of his shoulder, but it drew blood. Mriy was already in full run by the time the knife hit. Rrumlau yelped and lost his grip on his rifle with his trigger hand. He dropped it to the snow when Mriy barreled into him as he tried to turn.

Rrumlau was a classic brute. He had twenty kilos on Mriy at the least, and was younger by a full hand of years—his fighting prime. But Mriy had stolen the initiative, first blood, and the upper position in the brawl. Soora had been built like Rrumlau. As he tried to buck and shove at her shoulders and hips, she realized that he fought much like her brother as well. Mriy let him push and struggle beneath her, shifting her weight and leverage so that he could not rise from the snow. With gravity aiding her, she landed heavy swipes to the sides of Rrumlau's head, narrowly avoiding the bites he attempted in defense.

They grappled in the snow for minutes, until Mriy managed to kick off her boots and get her hind claws into Rrumlau's flanks. That rendered his legs flailing and useless and started to compress his abdomen, robbing him of breath. The larger azrin tired quickly from that point, struggling for breath and clawing effectually at Mriy's arms and face. With her toe claws dug in, the battle of arms only needed a stalemate from her end. As Rrumlau fought for air, his struggles turned entirely defensive. Mriy picked her way through his guard and pounded him until he was dazed and limp.

Rolling off the heavier fighter, Mriy fumbled in the snow until she found the dropped blaster rifle. It was cheap and lightweight, nothing like the ordinance Tanny procured for the *Mobius*. She crawled over to Rrumlau, who was now helpless on his back, trying to regain lost breath and staunch the bleeding in his sides. She aimed the rifle down, right where she judged his heart to be.

Mriy listened. For the first time since the blood rush of combat began, she noticed her surroundings. The hum of snow-roller engines had faded into the distance and was gone. If she was lucky, she could follow the trail. They might double back for her, or stop and wait if they thought pursuit was lost.

Rrumlau spat up at her. Given his struggles to fill his lungs, she gave him the barest credit for managing to spit into her face. But it was a mistake. Mriy hissed and tightened her finger on the trigger. But it didn't fire. The last little bit, the final squeeze that would send a burst of plasma to incinerate Rrumlau's heart, would not come.

Light poured from the door of the domicile, spilling across the snow. Azrin voices shouted demands and threats. Mriy tried once again to pull the trigger, but couldn't bring herself to do it. She had counted on the rebels' beliefs to protect her—that they would not kill one of their own kind. How could she show clear proof that she was less noble?

Mriy flipped the rifle around and brought the butt end down on Rrumlau's upper jaw. The crack that sounded was payback for his spitting on her. A glance at the rebels pouring from the domicile told her that there was no escaping. She might kill a few, but they wouldn't hesitate to kill her in self-defense at that point. Letting the rifle slip from her grasp, Mriy collapsed onto her back in the snow.

Footsteps crunched through the snow toward her. "By your place in God's heaven, what came over you?" Hraim asked as he loomed over Mriy.

"They were my pack," Mriy mumbled, too exhausted in mind and body to lie. "They were *all* my pack. Even the damned dog."

❀ ❀ ❀

"We have to go back for her," Esper insisted. Her stomach lurched as the snow-roller took a turn, while she was twisted around watching behind them.

"We can't," Auzuma replied. It was just the two of them; Tanny drove the rebels' only other snow-roller and had Kubu with her.

"They'll kill her," Esper said. "She betrayed them."

"Those rebels are true believers," Auzuma replied. "They know their Book. 'You shall not kill kin.' Most of my people take it to mean not to kill within the clan. But those rebels, they hold to the old interpretation. We are all God's children, so they won't kill another azrin."

"My species has that one, too," Esper replied. "It's worded a little less ambiguously, and they still break it all the time."

"I've met few pious humans," Auzuma said. He swerved the snow-roller around a fallen tree, causing Esper's gorge to rise. She gave up on watching the second snow-roller and the path behind them. "We heard the word of the same God, but we followed it better. We have had no flood, no great plagues—yes, I've read your Bible. Our commandments numbered just six, and we followed them better than your kind ever did."

"But what if they're not as pious as you think?"

"Then Mriy will die."

"Right! So we have to go—"

"No," Auzuma said. His easy banter was gone. His pronouncement carried the weight of finality. "If Mriy needs saving, it will be the Yrris Clan who goes back for her—with a ship. Not us."

Mriy didn't remember being dragged indoors, but she recognized the scent of the rebels' hearth fire before she opened her eyes. The sap from the green pine wood gave off a distinctive aroma. She would have liked to take a good sniff of the room, but feared that she might alert her captors that she was awake; instead she let the smells around the room waft to her. Hraim was here, along with Rrumlau and four other rebels.

She lay facedown on the dirt floor, arms pinned behind her. Ropes at her wrists and elbows kept her forearms pressed together and her shoulders straining in their sockets. Her legs were splayed, pulled in opposite directions—probably tied to stakes. It would have been a comical parody of some of the worst locally produced holovids if it weren't so painful. The only solace she could take was that they left her arms—and claws—facing upward; it meant they didn't intend to violate her before she died.

A bare toe prodded her ribs, and Mriy realized she was unclad. "She's awake."

Hraim knelt beside her. "Well, well. Looks like our friend is faking." A thin-clawed slap left trails of fire across Mriy's face.

She opened her eyes. "You are sad relics, living in dead days."

"And you're a traitor to your kind." Rrumlau spoke with his jaw clenched. Mriy took grim satisfaction knowing that she'd broken it.

"What do we do with the human-lover?"

"She's as good as human. Just kill her."

"Make her pay, first."

Hraim pressed her head to the floor and stared into Mriy's eyes. "No. She's still azrin. We don't kill kin. But I think, if she wants to be part of a human pack, we oughtta help her."

Rrumlau strutted into view. He bent low and held out a hunter's tool, a pair of iron pliers that looked old enough to have been in his family for generations. They were used for taking trophies from a kill. Speak to any hunter who wore a necklace of teeth or claws, and he could pull such a tool from his pocket to show you. Mriy owned a little-used pair that she kept on board the *Mobius*.

Hraim held out a short piece of a tree branch that hadn't been stripped of bark. It was thick as her forearm. "Open up. This is the last favor we do you."

Mriy felt an instinctive urge to resist, to thwart any effort her captors made. But she knew the truth of it, and realized why her hands were tied behind her, where her captors had easy access. It was accept their offer, or suffer through the pain with nothing to bite on while they declawed her.

With a growl, she snapped her jaws down on the wood, giving a resentful glare as she did. But Rrumlau just laughed, and Hraim tied a cord around one end of the wood and looped it behind her head before trying the other. He wasn't securing it so Mriy didn't spit it out; he was forcing her jaws wide until she could barely bite down at all. Her protests came as inarticulate grunts.

Rrumlau turned and swiveled an ear toward her. "What's that? I don't understand human."

Her captors pressed Mriy firmly to the floor. Try as she might, with no leverage she couldn't stop them from unclenching her fists and forcing her claws out, one by one. In gentler fashion, it was the same trick a mother used to file a child's claws. But one by one, those pliers clamped down and pulled. Mriy screamed into the wooden bit between her teeth as searing pain blazed at each finger, each adding to the misery of the last. One by one, bloody claws were pitched into the hearthfire as Mriy watched through eyes swimming with tears.

Ten fingers. Eight toes. She could barely whimper by the time they finished.

Rrumlau patted her on the cheek. "That wasn't so bad, was it?" He opened and closed the pliers with a rusty grating noise. The wet tips gleamed in the firelight.

Mriy grunted. Her jaw ached, and she was dribbling spittle onto the dirt. She wanted to goad them into hearing what she had to say, just so they would take the bit away.

Rrumlau cocked his head. "What's that? You say humans don't have fangs? Why... I think you may be right about that."

Mriy's eyes went wide. She'd had enough. Hadn't they done enough?

With frantic urgency, she struggled against her bonds. A knee came down hard on her back, across her already-strained shoulders. Hands gripped either side of the wooden bit and pulled her head back. Mriy might have been stronger than any one of them, maybe even Rrumlau. But tied up, beaten, and exhausted, she offered only feeble resistance.

Her breath quickened as she saw the pliers coming. Rrumlau took his time. She felt the wiggle in her jaw, the tug, the pain. The pulling brought her head forward despite the rebel holding her back. Then her head bobbed back and she tasted hot blood in her mouth. Spots swam before her eyes. Rrumlau waved the tooth with its bloody roots in front of her eyes before tossing it into the fire.

Three more times, and each time Mriy wished she was weakling enough to pass out from the pain.

When they finally untied the bit from her mouth, it slid out easily; no canine fangs impeded its exit. When they cut her bonds, she lay limp; no strength remained in her muscles.

"Kill... me."

Hraim hooked a foot under her side and rolled Mriy onto her back. "You're going to die, but we won't kill you. You're going to die like a human. Alone in the wilderness. Unable to hunt. I'd have shaved you bare like a human, but freezing's an easy way to go. You'll find water, if you don't lie there and give up. You're going to starve—starve in a forest filled with game you're too weak and harmless to kill."

Rrumlau dragged her outdoors by the wrists. The cold felt wonderful, the snow numbing her wounds. She made a point of hiding that revelation, lest they bring her back inside. But it appeared that they had other plans for their shelter. Mriy watched the smoke as it burned.

Hraim was the last to address her before the rebels left. "Mriy Yrris, in your last moments, I hope you repent. Think about what you've done, and the mistakes that brought you to this end."

Mriy knew already. Hraim, Rrumlau, and all the rest had shown her with perfect clarity. She should never have come back.

Carl stood at the back of the viewing room in the *Yinnak*, killing time along with a host of Mriy's relatives and his own goddamn wizard. The box he flipped idly and caught, again and again, was worth 25,000 terras to whoever was slumming around astral space at the edge of the system. Mort could trust the azrins for a few hours—tops—and be back to watch the end of the contest. Instead, Mort sat there stuffing local sushi in his face, explaining the nuances of Napoleonic warfare as the holovid showed the Battle of Waterloo.

The only thing that kept Carl from losing his cool and screaming Mort's bloody head off was the fact that the other 25,000 had been paid up front. It took a lot to upset the captain of a ship who'd just put 25,000 terras in his pocket, but a thin thread dangling the other half toward a black hole was enough to do it. Just then he wished Mort actually worked *for* him, so he could threaten to fire him.

Carl had always hated any math more complicated than a split of loot from a job. He piloted by gut and let the computers handle the fiddly bits with numbers. But there was an answer to one question he needed: how long did he have before he couldn't make his drop on time. The nameless weasel who'd given him the box and paid him had insisted that late was as good as never delivered. That meant that the ship out there waiting was on a tight deadline. Get to the coordinates and astral depth any later than 5:00PM, November 21 Earth Standard, and that ship would be gone.

It was 3:21PM. Less than two hours away. Planetary rotation kept it from being much past daybreak locally, but Earth Standard didn't care about local sunlight. The box was as light as the client had claimed, made from some advanced plastic composite without any locking mechanism visible. Whatever was inside was probably a lot of trouble, as were the nameless weasel and whoever was paying him the other half of his 50,000. But whatever was inside was also probably pretty damned valuable—maybe even worth more than the 25,000 even accounting for whatever trouble it brought with it.

Carl made an executive decision. He nudged one of the glass-eyed azrins watching holovids with Mort. "Hey, got a comm I can borrow?"

He'd guessed well, and this Yrris understood English. "Sensor station, door before the cockpit."

"Thanks," Carl replied, patting the azrin on the shoulder as he left the viewing room. Sometimes a vague, offhanded request with no context could get people to agree to pretty stupid things.

Carl settled himself into the seat at the sensor station. It took a couple minutes to reset the language to English, but it was a variant of a computer system used across half of ARGO space, so Carl muddled his way through it. Relays, proxies, and ghost comm IDs didn't fall under Carl's list of skills. He settled for opening an account on a local omni exchange under a false name and residence, then began his text-only message.

AGRO patrol. I hav loyal message. Smuggel ship wait on border. Much wanted. I am loyal, no criminal. You find, keep Meyang saif. Love For Meyang!

Cross-referencing with his own datapad, Carl attached the coordinates and astral depth the nameless weasel had provided. Hopefully the false ID and crummy spelling and grammar would convince the garrison busybodies that it was a local ratting someone out. They'd never believe that whoever sent the message was innocent, but that made it all the more likely they'd send someone to check it out.

Carl reset the comm panel to azrin and headed back to see who won the Battle of Waterloo.

It was approaching noon local time when Roddy caught Carl on the comm.

"*Boss, we got a problem,*" Roddy said. Carl could hear the nerves in his voice. Either that laaku wasn't drunk enough, or something was going badly.

Carl looked around the room at his azrin hosts; none of them were paying attention. "Dump it. Line's clear enough."

"*You remember those Harmony Bay bastards?*" Roddy asked.

"How could I forget them?" Carl replied, covering his non-comm ear with a hand to block out the noise of the Yrris' latest selection, a pre-ARGO laaku martial arts vid. "Not every day someone comes that close to dusting us."

"*The* Bradbury *just entered orbit around Meyang.*"

"That's..." Carl struggled for a word. "...ominous. How much of a signature have we got on the ground?"

"*This comm is about the only thing running right now,*" Roddy replied. "*I even opened the* Mobius *up and turned off life support. We'll be scrubbing local air through the filters for weeks, but our EM signature is zilch.*"

"Good call," Carl said. "We can hang tight until the crew gets back, wait for them to be on the other side of the planet, then—"

"*Is that* Eight Fists, No Waiting *I hear in the background?*"

"Yeah."

"*I'll be right over,*" Roddy said. "*Haven't seen that since I was a kid.*" The comm clicked and went silent. Two minutes later, the laaku was parking himself between two of Mriy's cousins, buying a welcome by sharing from his six-pack of Earth's Preferred.

Carl stewed and watched the laaku join his wizard in thrall to the holovid. Under normal circumstances, he'd have been all for leaking some coolant pressure over a few hours of mindless holovid action. It was early laaku holovid, so the quality was low, but the action was top notch. Unfortunately, there was too much action in real life hanging over him for Carl to let loose. It came as a relief when the Yrris hunting pack arrived back. Everyone went outside to witness the return.

There was a hullabaloo, with all the Yrrises celebrating Mriy's nephew and his pack of ringers. When Carl saw the size of the azrins who'd gone with him and then considered who Mriy had dragged along, he realized she probably never stood a chance. The elk was a dead elk. It looked stupid, colored up like some cave painting. Its neck lolled and was clearly broken. Carl's stomach was just as glad that it wasn't drenched in blood.

Carl pulled Seerii aside as the initial jubilation died down. "So, Mriy loses. Can we go round up her pack and get out of here?"

"She might not forgive you," Seerii replied, keeping her voice low. "But you should take her from here when she returns. By law she is welcome. By all other measures, she is not."

"We just wait here?" Carl asked. "How long should they be?"

"There is no way to be sure, but they should have been tracking the winning pack. Not long, I imagine."

Seerii was right, but for all the wrong reasons. It wasn't long before two snow-rollers thundered into the base camp, pulling up beside the *Yinnak*. There were two occupants in each, which by Carl's simple math, put them one pack member short. "Where's Mriy?" he shouted over the noise of the combustion engines, before someone cut power to them.

"We ran into rebels hiding out in the hunting grounds," Tanny replied, hopping down from the snow-roller. She wasn't wearing any boots.

"We've got to go after her," Esper added. She wasn't wearing boots either, and there was blood at her wrists.

"The hell happened to you girls?" Carl asked.

"We got captured," Tanny said. "They're not exactly pro-human, if you know what I—is your hair *blue*?"

Carl's face froze. "That *bastard*! He said he fixed it." Carl looked at the backs of his hands—brown. He squinted and pushed an eyebrow into his field of view—brown. He tried holding his datapad up as a mirror, but the black surface didn't deal well with color in reflections.

"Quit it," Esper scolded. "Those rebels have Mriy. She was holding one of them off to cover our escape. She said they won't kill her, but she needs *us* to rescue her."

"Roddy, fire up the engines," Carl said. "Everyone else, get on board. Seerii, I'd love to say it's been nice, but your planet is a shithole and its inhabitants have been pissing me off since I got here."

"How dare you—" Seerii snarled, flexing her claws.

Mort put a warning hand on her arm as he passed by. "Wouldn't try that," he cautioned.

"What about that Harmony Bay ship?" Roddy asked.

Esper's eyes went wide. "What Harmony Bay ship?"

"We'll worry about the *Bradbury* if we have to," Carl said. "I don't believe in coincidences, but that doesn't mean we can't get lucky once in a while. We're finding Mriy and getting the hell out of this system."

They didn't have much to retrieve before lifting off. Mort had brought a few personal effects that he refused to depart without, but that was the bulk of it. They were closing up the ship minutes later.

"Wait," Auzuma shouted as the cargo ramp went up. Roddy hit the control button and stopped it. "Give this to Esper." He handed Roddy a book in Jiara script. The title just said: Book.

"Will do," Roddy replied and closed the bay door.

Tracks led from the burned-out ruin of the rebel compound. One set were azrin footprints, another the twin lines left by snow-rollers. Mriy followed the latter. Though there was little chance of the rebels coming back for her, Mriy didn't want to wait for rescue. She had enough fat on her to weather the cold without winter gear; under the daytime sun, it was even refreshing. The wind whipped a dusting of snow from the ground. Tiny crystals of ice caught in her fur and froze there.

Years of training as a hunter, a warrior, and a Silver League fighter went into simply keeping her balance as she set down one foot, then the other. That two-step repetition was all she needed to follow the tracks. They would hate her at the Yrris clanhold. Hrykii would mock her. Yariy would gloat. Seerii would send her away. And she would go. And she would not return. Never return.

One foot. Other foot.

It had been foolhardy to return and try to wrest her old position back.

One foot. Other foot.

But Esper, Tanny, and Auzuma had gotten away. Or at least she hoped they had.

One foot. Other foot.

She caught the scent of a hare on the wind. In daydream, she would catch it, crush it between clawless fingers, tear at its flesh with her incisors, carefully avoiding the tender, bloody holes in her mouth.

One foot. Snow.

The ground rushed up and slammed into Mriy. The powder cushioned her fall. Her breath melted a tiny area around her mouth and nose. Blood stained the snow.

❁ ❁ ❁

Tanny took the pilot's chair, adjusting it mid-flight and complaining all the while about what Carl and Roddy had done to it in the three days she'd been gone. Carl had offered to fly, since Tanny was half-frozen, wounded, and didn't have any boots. In typical marine fashion, she'd brushed those concerns aside as inconsequential to the mission.

"How far is it?" Carl asked. He stood behind the copilot's seat, where Esper had taken position, watching out the forward window as the Mobius flew with its nose angled down for better visibility.

"Not far," Tanny replied.

Esper pointed. "I recognize that hilltop. We camped within sight of it the first night. But we just took off." She was chewing on some of Mort's leftover sushi after healing her wrists.

"There's a reason they build these things," Carl said. "Walking long distances outdoors is for animals. Just ask Roddy about Phabian; you can live there your whole life without setting foot outdoors. That retrovert stuff is bullshit."

Esper held a hand over her mouth as they ducked over hills and mountains with the ship's attitude and altitude making it appear they were going to crash any second. She was still new to this whole business. Motion sickness was something she was going to have to learn to deal with.

"There it is," Esper said. To her credit, she'd kept her eyes open when shutting them would have made the effects go away. After all, none of the G-forces were overcoming the ship's gravity.

A plume of smoke rose through the trees. "I'll man the guns," Carl said. "Esper, take Mort to the cargo bay. We might need unconventional firepower, and you might need to heal Mriy, depending on what kind of shape she's in."

"What if they're not willing to negotiate?" Tanny asked.

"With Mort?" Carl scoffed.

"Right," Tanny replied. A failed negotiation with the ship's wizard wasn't something one walked away from.

But all their preparations were in vain, except for Esper's. The camp was burned and abandoned. Tracks led off deeper into the mountains, and if they had wanted to, the *Mobius* could have hunted them down. But the crew spread out along the compound and found what they were looking for.

Mriy had collapsed in the snow, less than a kilometer down the trail left by the snow-roller escape. It was Kubu's nose that found her; the white of her fur made her nearly invisible. When Tanny rolled her over to check her vitals, they noticed the blood. There were gashes on her sides and face, and all along her arms. What drew attention their were the bloody tips of each finger and the red all around her muzzle. Her eyes fluttered open, then shut tight against the glare.

"Get her something to eat," Esper ordered, putting her hands on Mriy's chest. But Mriy shook her head. In obvious pain, she opened her mouth and showed the raw sockets where her canine teeth had been pulled. "Oh Lord!"

"Mort, levitate her and be gentle about it," Carl ordered. "We'll get this sorted out in the Black Ocean. We've got a ship up there that's getting closer by the second."

❀ ❀ ❀

"The *Bradbury* is closing on us."

Carl swore under his breath. "How long to break atmosphere?"

With a quick check of the scanners, Tanny shook her head. "We're not winning this race."

Carl ran down the hall to the common room. "Mort! What are the prospects of astral from atmosphere?"

The grizzled wizard hung an eyebrow low as he scratched his chin. "I don't like that prospect one bit. Rather get boarded and roll up my sleeves for the fight."

At that moment, Esper backed out of Mriy's quarters, shutting the door softly behind her. "She's in bad shape. If she was human, I think she might have died already. I gave her a trickle of healing, just enough to stop the bleeding. But she's in no shape to eat anything right now."

Carl held up a hand. "Great. You keep on that. We'll figure something out once we get away from the—"

"No!"

Carl blinked.

Esper stood toe to toe with him. "Harmony Bay is the leading medical supplier in the galaxy. The *Bradbury* will have better medical staff than anyone planetside or most of the colonies we visit. I can't magic Mriy up new teeth or claws. She needs a med bay."

Carl shook his head and headed for the cockpit. "I don't have time for this right now. We'll get Mriy to a med facility... maybe Sindra III. She's tough. She'll pull through."

Esper followed him to the cockpit. A comm came in just as he settled into the copilot's chair. "*Vessel Mobius, this is Captain Yasmira Dominguez of the* Bradbury. *You are in possession of property that belongs to us. Cut your engines and prepare for docking.*"

The ship shook gently. Tanny twisted the flight yoke left and right, but the *Mobius* didn't maneuver. "Shit. They locked on a tractor beam."

Carl reached for the comm, but Esper leaned past and put a hand over it. "Hand over their thingy, the one we were supposed to deliver."

"If I'd have known it was them, I never would have taken the job."

Esper raised her voice. "That doesn't matter. Give it back and bargain for them to fix up Mriy."

Tanny pulled her hand away. "It's a nice thought, but we can't trust them."

"I thought Captain Carl Ramsey could talk his way out of anything. Huh?"

He met her glare, and she must have seen something there, because the bluster drained from her in an instant. Not taking his eyes off hers, Carl reached out and powered down the engines. "Yeah. I can."

❂ ❂ ❂

They always underestimated her hearing. Days spent planetside had sensitized Mriy to the various noises on the ship. Before the hunt, her ears had learned to ignore the droning of the holovid, arguments in the common room, and Mort's snoring. It was the key to staying sane in close quarters aboard ship. But hunting brought back that sharpness of ear that listened for cracking of twigs and the sudden change in birdsong that signaled a predator's presence. Even through the door of her quarters, she could strain and make out every word of the argument in the cockpit. God's favorite niece was going to convince Carl to surrender so that Harmony Bay could treat Mriy's wounds.

The wonderful thing about every part of Mriy's body hurting was that nothing she did could make her feel worse. Pains would shift and vie for attention, but overall the effect was the same. With a grunt of effort, she sat up. From there it was easy. A few shuffling steps to the door. A ginger grasp to turn the handle. A shoulder to shove it open.

Mort stood waiting in the common room, staff in hand. "Egads! Are you delirious? Get back to bed. You're in no condition to—"

"Must. Stop. Carl."

Mort played the old fool much of the time, but he was not. Instead of arguing with her, he offered his shoulder and helped Mriy's faltering footsteps up to the cockpit.

The argument over whether to surrender continued as they approached. The hum of engines died away. "Yeah, I can," Carl said with typical smugness. He thought himself without peer. He thought he could lie away any trouble.

Had Mriy not been just like him with similar blind faith in her prowess? "Don't. Not worth... it." Speaking with missing teeth, she sounded like a child. She wiped at her mouth and found blood on the back of her hand.

"Good heavens! Mriy, what are you doing up?"

Mriy shrugged aside Esper's attention and put her face close to Carl's. "No."

To his credit, Carl didn't shy or look away, not even when Mriy parted her lips to let him see the bloody wreck left from the rebels' handiwork. "You sure about this? These bastards have the tech to fix you... real teeth, real claws, good-as-new fixed."

There was a nagging temptation. A good half of Carl's schemes worked out. He might be able to convince them to patch her up, to let them all go unharmed—though probably without payment. From the bits and pieces, she had gathered there was something Carl owed them, but that wasn't the point. The question was whether she could ask them to stand in the line of fire for her... again. "Not. Worth. Don't trust."

Tanny cleared her throat. "Well, that's just peachy, but we're still caught in their tractor beam."

"Esper, get Mriy back to bed. Mort, think you can disrupt that tractor beam without killing off half the ship's systems?"

"No, but I may be able to do one better. Let them drag us close." Mort pushed past Esper and Mriy, staff tapping along the ground as he strode back to the common room.

Carl called after him. "I hope you know what you're doing!"

"Of course he does," Esper muttered, so softly that she probably didn't expect even Mriy to have heard her.

Mort began his chanting. Whatever language he used, the earring that translated every other language in the galaxy threw its hands up in despair. The light changed in the common room. Though it took a great effort to crane her neck, Mriy peered up through the domed ceiling to watch astral gray replace the black and stars of realspace. The sight had never failed to unnerve her, but this time she was too weary to care.

The *Bradbury* was oriented so that it was visible through the canopy. Even as the *Mobius* sank into the astral, it never wavered. It couldn't have been more than a hundred meters away.

Carl shouted from the cockpit. "Mort, you daft old shit! You're bringing them with us! This isn't how escapes work!"

Trusting that Esper would mind her footing for her, Mriy kept watch on the sky. The gray deepened and darkened. It took on an aspect of violet. All the while, the *Bradbury* remained fixed in place, towed along with Mort's magic.

From the cockpit, the comm blared. "*Vessel Mobius, I don't know how you're doing this, but you have thirty seconds to return us to realspace or we will open fire, cargo or no cargo.*"

Mort gave a wave at the ship on the other side of the glassteel dome, and the tone of his chanting shifted. The purplish tinge of astral space faded to the accustomed gray, and this time, the *Bradbury* faded from view, no longer following in their wake.

Cupping a hand to his mouth, the wizard shouted to the cockpit. "All clear. Let's see their star-drive gizmo dig them out of *that* mess!"

As Mriy let Esper settle her back into bed, she could hear Carl and Tanny arguing over the course to plot that would put them farthest from Harmony Bay's influence. Or the nearest medical facility. Or someplace remote. Or a place with xeno-cosmetic facilities. Mriy let her head sink into the pillow and closed her eyes. Not everything hurt. Her heart was at peace. She was home.

❀ ❀ ❀

Mriy looked at herself in the mirror. Everything in her mouth was sore, and the taste was strange. She opened wide and inspected the ceramite implants, trying to remember what her natural teeth had looked like. If there was a difference, she couldn't tell. The cosmo-surgeon had done his job.

She flexed the claws of her left hand, wincing as the sheaths flexed around tender tissue. Her false claws were a silvery black, made of a material she couldn't pronounce in English. They were sharper than her old ones, and would need to be replaced every few years, depending how roughly she treated them. It would be days yet before she was willing to try them on anything tough like fresh meat. It was strange to think that there were parts of her that were no longer her own.

A tentative knock at her door meant that Esper had come to check on her again. "Enter," Mriy said, wincing in anticipation of a pain that didn't come as she spoke. It was a promising sign.

Esper opened the door and smiled. "You're looking much better this morning."

"I am feeling better. But the answer is still 'no.'"

"You'd feel ship shape after a big meal," Esper countered. It was a sweet gesture. While useless to the point of infuriating in the wild, Esper was of great use elsewhere. Simple kindness was something Mriy had taken to underestimating.

She sat down on the bed and gestured for Esper to join her. The human joined her, sitting a meter away. Being shirtless was taboo among human women, but not at all so for azrin. She slid over and wrapped her arms around Esper, who stiffened for a moment before relaxing. "You have been a better friend than I deserve. Young as you seem at times, you are my elder, and wise in ways I don't see easily. My wounds pain me, and I know you could ease them. But I will recover, and my recovery will reinforce the many lessons I've learned since the hunt. I have no mother who wants me. My clan is foreign to me now. But I have two sisters and three brothers instead—and a dog, I suppose."

Esper tried to put her arms around Mriy but could not come close to reaching. She stopped trying and settled for being held, leaning against Mriy's chest. "I've thought about going home, too. I don't think it would go well. For better or worse, this is my home now. You all are my family."

"I only wish I could have seen Neep while I was there," Mriy said softly. She winced and her ears twitched. That was something she hadn't meant to mention.

"Who is Neep?" Esper asked.

Mriy swallowed. Esper was family; she would understand. "He was my pet. I was two when I named him; Neep is a childish name."

"What kind of pet?" Esper prodded. There was a sweetness in her question; humans had such weaknesses for pets. It explained much of what Kubu got away with, despite being able to speak and understand.

Mriy sighed. "A hyoba—a tiny hominid. They... they look like little humans, just knee high. Neep is the noise they make, like a dog's bark. I don't mean anything by having one. I know they're illegal, but I was only—"

Esper laughed and pulled herself from Mriy's embrace. "That sounds adorable."

❂ ❂ ❂

Captain Carl Ramsey slumped down onto his bed and leaned back against the wall. With datapad in hand, he got back to a little side project he had started working on. It was time to update the notes for his eventual memoir.

We cleared out of Meyang before those shits from Harmony Bay found their way out of astral. I never imagined that the ship I ratted out to ARGO would be one of theirs. I get plenty of shit around here for bad plans that we pull off anyway, but this was a damn fine plan if I do say so... we just got unlucky.

Mriy was in bad shape, but she's tougher than composite steel. We needed to get her to a medical facility, someplace where we wouldn't worry about Harmony Bay grabbing us. Normally we stick to the edges of society—the borderlands, the systems just outside ARGO space, the little pockets of savage space without inhabited systems. Even Meyang was uptown for us. But Roddy figured that with our scraped-clean records, we could afford a trip to Phabian and found a doctor on one of the outer worlds that was willing to work for cheap on an azrin. I hope we never have to tell Mriy that he was a veterinary specialist. Since we blew our stolen take from the delivery for the weasel, she shouldn't be asking too many nosy questions about how we pulled it off.

I'm thinking that it's time we lay high for a bit, since lying low's gotten us in so much trouble lately. We can take our respectability and see how far we can push it before we piss someone off.

Mort's beside himself with glee that Esper managed to summon fire while she was out hunting with Mriy. I guess it goes to show that wizards get what they want. I just hope she never finds out who was in that confessional. Maybe I can hold that over him to get him to finally turn my hair back to its original color. I just hate to think what he'll come back with if I start fighting dirty.

Kubu's going to be a problem, sooner or later. He's behaving better, but he's going to bankrupt us on food alone. Not to mention the fact that he's putting on ten kilos a week and it's all going into muscle and bone. There isn't a flabby bit of that mutt. In a month, he's going to be bigger than Mriy, and in three I'm wondering how he's going to fit through doors. I think "Mommy" is going to have to make a hard choice soon about his future.

I've still got my suspicions about how this whole business started. It was so seat-of-the-pants at the time that none of us had a chance to pick it apart and see if the pieces fit. Damn convenient that Mriy had someone point her to a relative in need of rescue, one who just happened to be the perfect key to unlock her old life if it had played out like she expected. She never said who tipped her off. I wouldn't be half surprised if *it was Mriy who hired that bounty hunter in the first place. I'd never be able to prove it, but if she did, she's been learning something around here.*

Carl paused and reread the last few paragraphs. With a frown, he scanned back and reread a few previous entries. Dreams of publishing his life's story someday and living off the holovid deal evaporated before his eyes.

"If anyone reads this, I'm a dead man," he muttered to himself, then deleted the file.

Thanks for reading!

You made it to the end! Maybe you're just persistent, but hopefully that means you enjoyed the book. But this is just the end of one story. If you'd like reading my books, there are always more on the way!

Perks of being an Email Insider include:

- Notification of book releases (often with discounts)
- Inside track on beta reading
- Advance review copies (ARCs)
- Access to Inside Exclusive bonus extras and giveaways
- Best of my blog about fantasy, science fiction, and the art of worldbuilding

Sign up for the my Email Insiders list at:
jsmorin.com/updates

Books by J.S. Morin

Black Ocean

Black Ocean is a fast-paced fantasy space opera series about the small crew of the *Mobius* trying to squeeze out a living. If you love fantasy and sci-fi, and still lament over the cancellation of *Firefly, Black Ocean* is the series for you!

Read about the Black Ocean series and discover where to buy at: blackoceanmissions.com

Twinborn Trilogy

Experience the journey of mundane scribe Kyrus Hinterdale who discovers what it means to be Twinborn—and the dangers of getting caught using magic in a world that thinks it exists only in children's stories.

Read about the *Twinborn Trilogy* and discover where to buy at: twinborntrilogy.com

Mad Tinker Chronicles

Then continue on into the world of Korr, where the Mad Tinker and his daughter try to save the humans from the oppressive race of Kuduks. When their war spills over into both Tellurak and Veydrus, what alliances will they need to forge to make sure the right side wins?

Read about the *Mad Tinker Chronicles* and discover where to buy at: madtinkerchronicles.com

About the Author

I am a creator of worlds and a destroyer of words. As a fantasy writer, my works range from traditional epics to futuristic fantasy with starships. I have worked as an unpaid Little League pitcher, a cashier, a student library aide, a factory grunt, a cubicle drone, and an engineer—there is some overlap in the last two.

Through it all, though, I was always a storyteller. Eventually I started writing books based on the stray stories in my head, and people kept telling me to write more of them. Now, that's all I do for a living.

I enjoy strategy, worldbuilding, and the fantasy author's privilege to make up words. I am a gamer, a joker, and a thinker of sideways thoughts. But I don't dance, can't sing, and my best artistic efforts fall short of your average notebook doodle. When you read my books, you are seeing me at my best.

My ultimate goal is to be both clever and right at the same time. I have it on good authority that I have yet to achieve it.

Connect with me online
On my blog at jsmorin.com
On Facebook at facebook.com/authorjsmorin
On Twitter at twitter.com/authorjsmorin

Made in the USA
Lexington, KY
18 December 2015